VOL   Vollmer, Matthew.

Future missionaries
of America.

$24.00

VOL   Vollmer,
Matthew.

Future
missionaries of
America.

$24.00

DATE	BORROWER'S NAME	

PRAISE FOR
FUTURE MISSIONARIES OF AMERICA

"Vollmer writes with great wisdom and insight about love, sex, and loss. He is particularly adept at depicting the thrilling experience of young love. Vollmer's narrative voice, reminiscent of T.C. Boyle, is also fully realized and very appealing-irreverent, vital, and bristling with vivid imagery and detail."
—***Library Journal*** Starred Review

"Matthew Vollmer has written a book that looks like America: it's big, funny, sad and hopeful; its ambition is to take over the world. I'm behind it one hundred per cent."
—**Daniel Wallace**, author of
Mr. Sebastian and the Negro Magician and *Big Fish*

"The characters who inhabit the hilarious, heartbreaking stories in *Future Missionaries of America* may be desperate; yet, for all their lost innocence, they have the capacity to celebrate life's joy and pain. At its best, Matthew Vollmer's writing bursts with a kind of ecstatic poetry."
—**Stewart O'Nan**, author of *Snow Angels*,
Songs for the Missing and *Poe*

"In prose that manages to be both precise and expansive, Matthew Vollmer tells compassionate stories of people forced to take action against difficult circumstances. This collection is bold and risky, written by a courageous new writer."
—**Chris Offutt**, author of *Kentucky Straight*

MORE PRAISE FOR
FUTURE MISSIONARIES OF AMERICA

"From the opening rhapsody to the final prayerful note, Matthew Vollmer's stories beautifully script the drama of a changed world in search of new words. Here you'll find the tensile strengths of realism set beside the radical innovations of experiment, the enduring power of the story reinvented for our new day. Virtuosic in its variations yet held together by a ballast of obsession, *Future Missionaries of America* has more range than most novels while doing brilliantly what stories do best: it deepens the mystery of others by making that mystery familiar."
—Charles D'Ambrosio, author of
The Point and Other Stories and *The Dead Fish Museum*

"There are large cracks in America, and a person can fall right down into them and never be seen again. Many of Matthew Vollmer's characters are on the verge of doing that. Wacked-out teenagers, mountain survivalists, Adventist evangelists, compulsive gamblers, estranged mothers, Goth girls, world-class skateboarders, English department dopeheads, broken-hearted dentists, every one of them caught in the midst of an unimaginable situation, usually involving inexpressible love or grief. I have never read any stories like these. Quite often, these stories are saying the unsayable."
—Lee Smith, author of *The Last Girls*

Future
Missionaries
of America

Stories by Matthew Vollmer

MACADAM CAGE

MacAdam/Cage
155 Sansome Street, Suite 550
San Francisco, CA 94104

www.MacAdamCage.com

Library of Congress Cataloging-in-Publication Data

Vollmer, Matthew.
  Future missionaries of America / by Matthew Vollmer.
    p. cm.
  ISBN 978-1-59692-312-6
  I. Title.
  PS3622.06435F88 2008
  813'.6—dc22

                              2008033632

Manufactured in the United States of America
10 9 8 7 6 5 4 3 2 1

Book design by Dorothy Carico Smith

The following stories have previously appeared in these publications:
"Future Missionaries of America," *Epoch*
"Oh Land of National Paradise, How Glorious Are Thy Bounties," *Paris Review*
"Two Women," *Tin House*
"The Digging," *Portland Review*
"Man-o'-War," *Colorado Review*
"The Gospel of Mark Schneider," *Virginia Quarterly Review*
"Second Home," *Fugue*
"Straightedge," *Salt Hill*
"Will & Testament," *Gulf Coast*

To KP and EV

Table of Contents

OH LAND OF NATIONAL PARADISE, HOW GLORIOUS ARE THY BOUNTIES

At midnight, Harper exits the dining room of the Old Faithful Inn and greets the distant geysers with a loud, resonant fart—*Take that, all ye fire-breathing monsters!*—then breaks into a run across the steamy, trembling ground. The moon is disarmingly bright, and Harper, still in his tux pants, shirt, bow tie, and name tag, heads for the shadows, chant-whispering: "I am alive, I am alive, I am the conqueror of all bad things." Hurling his body through space, he believes, will alter his chemistry, will help rearrange and therefore maybe understand those words that, just before dawn, streamed from the sticky earpiece of the employee-dorm pay phone, the voice on the other end—so steady, almost serene—informing Harper that his best friend, Wesley Morgan Montgomery, had not pulled through the coma—that he had died in his sleep.

Harper spent the rest of the day working a double (*somebody* had to fill Wes's shift), and as he delivered platters of dewy greens and loins of beast to people who had not died, he kept forgetting, then re-realizing, that Wes had—just like that—slipped into oblivion. Once, when he lost himself in the details of Wes's passing—the helicopter airlifting Wes's body from the bend in the road where the RV had struck him and where a hole in his head had opened and bled and refused to close—Harper spilled an entire tray of huevos rancheros for a table of very disappointed Midwesterners (Boilermakers, it appeared, from their sweats), who shook their big sad heads at him. Harper was tempted to think that head-shaking, when placed within the context of death, should seem pathetically trivial, and that knocking these same heads together would produce a highly satisfying sound, but then, from somewhere deep in his own head, he heard Wes's voice, saying, "What if you were a very hungry person with a big fat sad head, wouldn't you be a little pissed off after being crammed into a tour bus all day, breathing the stink of your fellow man, only to have your waiter dump your food on the floor?" So Harper forgave the head-shaking, shut his eyes, took a deep breath, counted to seven, and imagined what diving into Pocket Basin would feel like—that secret pool in the Firehole River where underground heat vents release bursts of warmth when feet smoosh into mucky bottom-ooze, and where clouds coast overhead like skiffs ferrying light across skies which only know how to be bright bright blue, and where sometimes there is a young woman swimming with you who encourages the shucking of swimsuits, a young woman named Abby who, over the past few weeks, you have fallen into an accidental kind of love with, regardless of the fact that falling in love with your best friend's lover isn't the most honorable thing in the world to be doing. But then again, maybe this is the finest tribute you can pay to a friendship, the *only* acceptable way to interact with a woman whose beauty and sarcasm and intellect you admired as she charmed your best friend first; a woman nobody could take their eyes off when she skipped into the employee cafeteria, her unbuttoned tux shirt exposing bellybutton ring and sports bra; a woman who's kept every dark secret you've told and who wept for the comatose Wes when you didn't have it in you; a woman who celebrates the way naked feels, whether it be in geyser steam, cotton sheets, or hot pools of mineral water, because when you're dead, who knows, maybe naked won't feel like this.

But now Abby and all warm river places are far, far away, so to stay warm Harper must keep running, and even though his black bow tie unhinges itself and flaps away into the night, he can't retrieve it, because that would be going back, and right now he's interested only in moving ahead, past all these welcoming moonlit portals which would burn you alive or, if one could stand the heat—*who knows?*—lead to worlds where warm, gooey life-forms fuse amoeba-style, regenerating forever and ever in tireless cheesy orgasms of light.

Twenty yards ahead, an old bison moseys through steamy bacteria slime, and Harper tells himself he's not afraid—*nothing to see here, keep moving*—though just last week an old bison of similar mass and mange plunged his horns into a New Jersey retiree and tossed him over a small pine tree. This bison, however, couldn't care less as Harper swooshes past, entering a cloud pouring from a troubled mouth in the ground, his nostrils gulping sulphur draughts as he savors the hot-wet, life-death pungencies now associated with the vocabulary of geothermals—a gurgling, plopping, whistling chorus best appreciated post twilight, because after the sun comes up, the tourists will return, emerging from tents, vans, and campers to begin their daily devastations, a series of performances which wouldn't be so unbearable if one were more like Wesley Montgomery, who'd stand among the sweaty throngs and robotic video cameras, not only watching with awe Old Faithful spewing her frothy load, but also watching with awe the watchers, a congratulatory look of *You all made it, the journey's over, old friends* spread across his face, and for a moment it would look as if he might embrace someone. In Wes' mind—as he offered to take snapshots of families posing before the plume—he *really was* playing gracious host to these poor souls who had saved their money for months, maybe even years, and traveled for days to reach this legendary wilderness of the American Sublime, this singular, glorious, fantastic realm of—

"Fuck *that*," Harper whispers, increasing speed, cherishing the sensation of not knowing where he's going, allowing his legs to make all the decisions, splatting through crusty patties of bison shit, taking shortcuts across glittering mineral crust, not caring if a leg should crash through to a searing world of pain on the other side, because he's got something to prove, which is that he's not afraid of searing worlds of pain; and when he glances into the sky to launch a thank-you to the always-benevolent Lord of Hosts—Who *must* be up there somewhere among and beyond the constellations—he trips and falls, skidding against the boardwalk, polyester ripping at his knees, splinters thrusting into his palms. But—imagining Wes cheering him on—he rolls and leaps up and regains his previous stride with an acrobatic fluidity, as if the fall were part of a practiced routine. He knows it should hurt more—his hands only slightly buzzing—but here in the Land of National Paradise, pain, like so much steam rising from the oozing wounds in the earth, evaporates—*whoosh*!—just like that. It's the healing distractions of nature's majesty, the annihilation—by water and fire—of all thoughts foul—and hup, there it goes *again*, another melty glob of rock sneezing smoke out its blowhole.

As Harper enters a field of black trees skeletonized by fires in eighty-eight, he considers sprinting toward the clean, well-lighted employee pub, where the sweet anesthesia of whiskey awaits, and where, though everyone's probably discussing with furrowed brows the fragility of life, things are unfolding as usual. It's fucking unbelievable, they'll say, burning their tongues on pizza and pouring draft beer down their throats. There will be grieving of course, because everybody knew Wes and will recall with fondness his repertoire of famous voices and how, when the managers weren't looking, he'd gobble leftover fries from the plates he'd lugged into the kitchen, and if somebody raised an eyebrow, he'd respond with a mouth full of food and a deadpan "What? You got something against other people's food?" Half-toasted employees will shake their heads in polite disbelief, and for the next few days, as they travel to their respective hospitality positions, they'll keep an eye out for wild RVs, but it won't stop Eddie from breaking a new game of pool or Heather and Tiffany from tipping back their sixth cocktail of the night while jabbering about the coming weekend, when a group of twenty-some hikers will climb to a remote glacial lake with a squishy green island in the center, where someone will lovingly present a baggie and a wooden pipe and pass around some grade-A hooch until they're all out of their heads and their clothes, and when they return Harper's friend Alan from Vermont will tell Harper that Alan's girlfriend, Jen from North Dakota, is planning an abortion but, no, that's not all, man, this isn't her first abortion, it's her *third*.

"God," Harper whispers, "God is our refuge and strength ever present in times of ...," wondering as he gazes across the rolling hills of smoking limestone if this qualifies as *trouble*, splashing through the Firehole River, a waist-high current threatening to take him down, but he twists and heaves and emerges on the other side, and almost trips again over a dead log, noting here that one tiny mistake and one could, quite easily, split one's head open, and that rubbery brains splurting out would leave one in a very different state of mind, and Harper wonders what if Wes had only had an itch in his groin before crossing the road or had remembered to look both ways or if only on his last morning Wes's alarm wouldn't have gone off or if, the night before the accident, Harper, instead of slipping quietly into Abby's bedroom, had thought to drag Wes out of his room, where he was sleeping his life away, to sit under the stars with a couple of beers because you know, Wes, even though we see each other every day and we grew up in the same town and rode our bikes off the same dirt embankments and sang hymns in the same church, we haven't talked over beer in a long time and there's a lot we should probably discuss—not the least of which are my feelings for the woman you love. "Oh yes, let's," Wes would've said (wouldn't he?), laughing and raising a foaming bottle to the sky, toasting the coincidence and dreaming up plans to provide for their collective joy. Sure, he might've slugged Harper in the stomach, but for the most part it would have been about forgiveness and staying up late and oversleeping just enough so that Wes would've had to run to work, by which time the RV of Death would have passed safely by.

But such thoughts are futile and dim and the boardwalk's coming to an end, so Harper savors the last rhythmic clomp of his shoes, a near profanity in this quietly hissing landscape. The sound of human feet running through this National Paradise Land is a sound he figures is near extinction, so hey, why not celebrate it? In fifty years, once his head has grown big and fat and sad like all the others, he'll return—maybe with Abby—to be trammed through the park in sterilized plastic pods, glum passengers gazing through insulated glass at plugged-up geysers spurting halfheartedly, sick animals collapsing around them, and everyone will wonder if such a travesty as ruining a National Paradise Land could ever be forgiven, everyone except the ones like Wes, who would say,

"Forget it. We were born to destroy, to *be* destroyed."

And here, Harper predicts, here is where a ghoulish Wes should appear out of nowhere to run alongside him, head wound and all, and perhaps he'll be wearing his tux, too, and offering whimsical advice from beyond the grave about how, for the love of God, one should let one rest in peace—but of course Wes does not appear out of nowhere, because once you enter nowhere, you're there for keeps. This realization, along with the subsequent acknowledgment of Life Going On, makes the already alien landscape even weirder—the smoking depressions in the ground, the crisp layers of lodgepole pines undulating in the moonlight, the random beasts of the field wandering through knee-deep puddles of algae— and suddenly the landscape seems so lucid, so *there*, so uncannily *real* and for a second Harper imagines that he might be the dream the landscape is having, that perhaps his body is lighter than the vapors it runs through. The inescapable bright white steam curdles and sways and forms, under the influence of moonlight, thousands of faces; faces like the hundreds of anonymous faces he serves each day; faces wearing the dough-faced grins of manta rays; faces thinking, *Where's my rainbow trout dammit?* and saying, "Don't call us *guys*, my wife isn't a *guy*"; the faces of Middle-Class Anglo Americans on Vacation, any of whom, at any time, could have a brain explosion.

And now, Harper intentionally crushes little violet-like flowers as he runs along the grassy banks of a stream winding beside the dormitories where most of the lights are out, though the light in his room is still burning because Kane from Alabama refuses to sleep in the dark. Harper won't ask why—he doesn't ask much of the slouching boy-man monstrosity, who fills empty water bottles with Copenhagen spit while drawing ink representations of eighteenth-century vampires, complaining that everybody here sucks and it's just a bunch of fuckin' dykes and fairies, and who, when Harper plays employee ambassador, saying, "Hey man, at least they're *trying* for the good things in life and searching for something bigger than themselves," mutters, "What the hell do you know, dumb ass," and Harper buttons his lip and turns over and tries to go to sleep, though for the past week all he's seen when he shuts his eyes is either the unconscious Wes with his face rearranged or the naked and smiling Abigail Brown, whom he was supposed to tell last week that maybe it would be in the best interests of all involved if they stopped seeing each other, an idea that didn't work because he kept ending up in her bed, where it was reverent and wild and pure and transcendent—until they stopped, of course, and were filled with a deep and poisonous silence.

"Ha!" Harper says aloud, marveling at the way his legs can just keep on going and going, it's like he's an incredible unstoppable futuristic running machine that screams *WAKE UP, ALL YE MOTHERFUCKING SLEEPERS—AND LIVE!* to all the rooms of the hotel, but nobody screams back at him, nobody wakes, and the tomb-dark windows make him think of graves, which make him think of the Great Beyond, which makes him wonder how many of these sleeping souls, on Resurrection Day, will be shot into Heavenly Paradise and whether or not he'll be chosen as one of the Very Elect, an idea that, if contemplated, might cause Harper to fall to the ground. Instead, he closes his eyes and keeps running, faster, faster, not even wondering if he'll smack into a tree or a car or a building or an elk or a bison, but simply eyes closed legs kicking, this I'm-not-afraid-to-run with-my-eyes-closed sensation propelling him forward, and in his head he's ascending

Middle Teton again, winding up gravelly trails, leaping streams, and when the mountain peak finally appears, a jagged fin iced with snow, swathed in cloud, he's traveling through a Zen painting and expects monks scouring the ground for psychedelic mushrooms but when he reaches the snowy top, where dead ancestral spirits supposedly reside in crystalline bliss, he finds he's alone.

Then WHOA it's cold fuzzy things kissing his face and he opens his eye to see the snow falling nonchalantly, flaky and soft. Like torn bits of icy paper, they cling to his eyelashes and when he squeezes them away with his eyelids they trickle down his face. Up in the sky, clouds have moved in but the moon's still in one corner and all across the land now snow is falling, settling on the roofs of the dormitories and the cafeteria and the tall triangular Old Faithful Inn, on the fur of the ambivalent bison, in the branches of lodgepole pines.

Finally, he reaches the dormitory where he lives and where a yellow light spills from the open door—*ahh yes, a sign of welcome*—and he leaps inside, his footsteps pounding out echoes and his breath reverberating off the cinder blocks as he turns a corner and finds the stairs and yanks himself up using the cold metal railing and then down another hallway and past the room of Robby from Arizona and Sam from Oregon, who, he sees in a peripheral flash, are still awake and kicking a Hacky-Sack around the room while Rachel from Texas stuffs marijuana into a bong pipe, and as he passes they call, "Harper! Hey Harper, where you been?" And his lungs burn as he gasps "running" without pausing because just thinking of what's going to happen gives him a hard-on midstride, a hard-on that will offer no solutions or consolations, but a hard-on that, nevertheless, must not go unused. He knows Abby's door will be cracked open and it is and he knows that she'll be asleep and it looks like she is so he quietly slides off his crusty tux shirt and pants and slips beneath the covers, wondering whether he should've taken a shower, though he knows she won't complain because she truly wants him no matter how badly he reeks. When she turns over he sees that she hasn't been asleep, but instead has been lying awake, apparently thinking about Wes and wondering where he, Harper, has been, because she was worried, she wanted to talk, she wanted to love him and postpone for a moment her dumbfounded loss. As they embrace he says, "Shh," thinking, *It will be better if we don't speak*, as their faces touch and with trembling lips his mouth finds hers while his hands work underneath the silk, touching her warm bountiful flesh, hastily unbuttoning and tugging and peeling away the clothes which are in the way of where he needs desperately to be. Soon, perhaps too soon, he's inside, and it's the familiar sensation of being *there*, ahhh yes, flesh against flesh, nervous systems broadcasting glorious messages to his brain, where suddenly, midthrust, he begins to dream, and in this dream he's flying, soaring over great dusty canyons with great waterfalls spilling over the brims, zooming above great blue lakes rippling like molten glass, and dive-bombing herds of bison; and there his friends are at Pocket Basin, the people who, like Wes and Abby and himself, found themselves packing up rusted cars and puttering across vast distances to reach this point of blessed exchange where they could find others who had done the same. A blurry-faced Wes is there and Abby is there—everyone is there—and they are all diving into the warm water and spitting it out of their mouths and some are standing above the water on the shore, where a hot spring begins bubbling. That's when Abby reminds him not to blast off inside her and so out he goes and when he does erupt he can't help but emit bursts of nervous laughter so loud that Abby says, "Shh," and cups her hand over his mouth.

Then they lie there together, bodies burning, temples touching. Tears—not his—drop onto his face and slide down his cheek; he knows Abby's thinking of Wes, maybe (and this is okay, maybe even preferable) thinking about how she wishes *he* was Wes. After a while, she's up, wiping off reproductive goop, and when there's a break in the clouds moonlight spills through the window. Suddenly it's all very sticky and stringy and disgustingly beautiful, this sex after death, but when she asks what's wrong he says, "I'm just tired"—a lie that feels like the truth. Every muscle burns as though torn and shredded. Breathing hurts; mucousy lungs rasp. He lies naked on the floor, wilting. Eyes closed, he tries to recover the dream but it's gone. He feels the quickened flopping of his heart against his chest and wonders if he's about to go wherever Wes went—to join him in a robe of light on a golf-green slope, with a flute of the finest champagne. But he can't see Wes, can't imagine his face. It's just the backs of his eyelids, which, he hypothesizes, are probably a thousand stars brighter than death's black hole.

He opens his eyes. Abby, in a grease-smudged T-shirt that looks a lot like one Wes used to wear, kneels beside him; a faint whistling streams from her nose. He wants to squeeze her good and hard and hang on 'til she makes him stop, though when her hand slides into his hair, he flinches. "Just be still," she whispers, "and let it out." He tries to obey, lying there quietly on the hard floor, patiently trying, but never managing, to cry. As Abby's fingernails scribble through his hair—a serene and thankfully indecipherable composition seeping in through his scalp—her soft, off-key humming fills the room. He can't recognize the song, but it sounds hopeful, and he likes it. Maybe, he thinks, it's a prelude for going out-side, an intro for an entering into dark and wind and snow. He imagines it now, the snow—*How beautiful! How weird and tranquil and terrible!*—like silence falling white, falling fast, covering and covering and covering the parts of the land that are cold. *And us out in it*—arms, hands, and faces flushed with the joyous stinging of flakes as they crash into flesh, with no words at all to say how it feels.

TWO WOMEN

1.

Two white women and a black baby stood on the shore of the river, watching the churning water where the keys had gone in. The younger woman had been holding the baby and spinning the keys on her finger, and the baby had been laughing, which, as always, caused the two women to laugh, and then, inexplicably, the key ring—which held keys to the Jeep, the A-frame, the shed, and the older woman's post office box—flew into the air, flashed in the light, and fell to the water.

The older woman, who planned on leaving that night with the baby to meet her husband, the poet, slid off her shoes and peeled off her shirt. Her bra was white. She pulled off her pants. Her panties were black. Her skin was tan and freckled. She replaced her sneakers. "I need goggles," she said, and went in.

"Do you want help?" the younger woman asked.

The older woman said nothing. She took a deep breath and slid deeper into the froth. She went in up to her chest. Her nipples hardened. She went under. The baby, thinking it a game, shrieked when she came up. She dove. She rose up. The baby squealed. She dove. Soon it was too dark to see. The older woman kept diving.

2.

The younger woman and her boyfriend had come from the city to the mountains for the summer. They had come to hike, fish, drink beer, and cook over a fire: to live in the woods in a tent. The younger woman's boyfriend had grown up in these mountains. He knew them. With a machete he sliced paths to caves and waterfalls. He started fires without matches. He recognized the tracks of various animals and identified distant birds. Sometimes when they were hiking, he'd pause to pluck the petal of a flower or the leaf of a tree, and chew it thoughtfully, as though it were providing him some message only his tongue could translate.

The boyfriend knew people. He talked a guy into giving him a job manning a ski lift, which, in summer, lifted not skiers but lazy hikers and the aged, both of whom brought sack lunches and cameras in backpacks. At the top, visitors marveled at the view: white sailboats winking on the blue lake, miles of mountains spreading out like folds in a great piney quilt.

Far below, the younger woman spent her days at a grassy lakeside park, reading books in flickering light beneath tall trees. Tourists arrived and videotaped the lake; swimmers sunned themselves on the beach. Groups of local preteens, toting rusty skateboards, whistled at her, their mushroom-legged jeans scuffing the grass, their hair gelled into the shapes of flames.

3.

The day she met the older woman, she'd been lying on a towel in the grass, staring at the lifeguard—a woman her boyfriend had dated in high school. The previous evening, the younger woman had been introduced to the lifeguard at a party with paper lanterns and hollowed-out melons filled with punch and chunks of fresh fruit—a party thrown by the lifeguard's parents. The lifeguard, hair streaked with gold, had worn a white sundress. She was so dark and willowy that when the younger woman, who'd just swallowed four lime Jell-O shots, stood next to her, she felt like a drunk, pudgy ghost. The lifeguard hugged her and grinned and told the boyfriend that oh boy, had he had picked a good one this time, they were perfect together, absolutely perfect, etc. The lifeguard was the kind of girl, the younger woman realized, who required attention. Unfortunately, no amount of attention could satiate her need for it, and the younger woman's boyfriend, someone who enjoyed giving attention indiscriminately, provided it.

"How do you make a tissue dance?" the boyfriend asked the lifeguard.

"Put a little boogie on it!" she exclaimed. She wrinkled her nose. She howled. The lifeguard wrapped her arms around the younger woman's boyfriend and squeezed him.

4.

Now the younger woman watched the lifeguard blow her whistle at a fat kid whose butterfly stroke had accidentally splashed an old lady in a bathing cap, watched as the lifeguard flirted with a tall, tanned boy with a rippling stomach. As she watched, she wondered if she could ever come to like the lifeguard. She wondered if she could somehow seduce her. She wondered if, given the right circumstances, in self-defense maybe, she could kill her.

"Hey," a voice said. "You're reading my book." An older woman with shoulder-length hair, curls still wet from a shower, stood above her. She wore khaki shorts, a blue T-shirt that said *MONTANA*, a silver bracelet, and butterfly earrings. Her legs, which were very tan, suggested she could run great distances. In her arms a black baby wore nothing but a diaper. He studied one of his dime-size nipples as though it were something he could peel away.

"Neepo," he said.

"You wrote this?" the younger woman asked, holding up

the book.

"I wish. I just owned it. I sold it back."

The baby squirmed. The woman dangled the baby by his feet. She lowered him to the ground. The baby squealed.

The woman explained that she and the baby lived here in the summer. In the winter she taught at a university out West. Her husband was a poet, with a residency in the desert. She was supposed to be writing, but looking after the baby was a full-time job.

The younger woman explained that she had come here with her boyfriend, who worked at the lift, and that they lived in a tent at the outskirts of town. The older woman tilted her head and frowned. The younger woman assured her it wasn't bad. The tent was made out of space-age material. There was a yellow glow inside. When the wind came through it rippled. The older woman wondered where they showered. The younger woman, aware of the dirt lining the ridges of her toes, the musk of her unwashed armpits, and the smudges of charcoal on her hands from putting out the campfire, explained that they took water from the river. Sometimes they showered in a motel down the road.

"Oh to be young," the older woman said. They stared out across the green grass. The lifeguard had crawled upon the tanned boy's shoulders.

"Do you think she's pretty?" the younger woman asked.

"Pretty? Yes." She paused. "Smart? No."

"You know her?"

"I've heard her talk. How can you not?"

The younger woman laughed. "Sometimes I wonder," she said, "and I don't mean this in a bad way...but what it would be like to be that...I don't know...unaware of yourself."

"Life would be easier," the older woman said.

"You could rule the beach with a whistle."

They laughed.

"Listen," the older woman said. "Would you like to earn some money?"

5.

"What's she doing?" the boyfriend asked. He squinted across the park, through the slanting light, at the lifeguard, who, still in her bathing suit, was cartwheeling across the beach. "She's crazy," he said, chuckling. He looked in the rearview and rubbed his teeth with a finger. "How was your day?" he asked.

"Fine," the younger woman said. She watched her boyfriend watching the lifeguard. She said nothing about the older woman and her baby.

"She has so much energy," the boyfriend said. The life-guard, who'd spotted their van, was now jogging toward them, her ponytail swinging behind her.

"Yes," the younger woman said, tearing a triangle of skin from a thumb with her teeth. "She sure does."

6.

They'd been asleep for two hours when the boyfriend's cell phone rang. The younger woman kicked him awake. The tent shivered as he fumbled for the phone.

"Okay, just calm down," he said. The younger woman knew, maybe by the tone of his voice, that it was the lifeguard. The boyfriend unzipped the curved tent fly and stepped out-side. He laced up his boots. He stirred the coals in the fire. "Oh my God," he said. "You're kidding. Nonononononono. Of course." The boyfriend beeped off the phone and poked his head through the fly. "Her boyfriend," he said. The younger woman pretended to be asleep. "He was in an accident. She needs a ride. Hey," he said. "I know you're not asleep. You're mad. *Listen*. Her boyfriend almost killed himself. I gotta go. You'll be okay?"

She nodded. He said, "I love you," and departed. The younger woman frowned. Her mouth dropped open. She listened to the van sputter away. She punched his sleeping bag. She cursed. Then, when she realized how far away from everything she was, and that she was alone, and that if her boyfriend, for some reason, became detained, or had a wreck himself, she'd be stuck here, she lay very still. She could hear something. Wind in the leaves? No. A rustling, just outside the tent. A beast? A thief? A pine tree. A muscle in her jaw began to spasm. Then a muscle in her leg. She held her finger up to the light coming through the space-age tent. The finger twitched.

Twitching, she knew, from surfing websites, was the first stage. In a few years, if the disease she was sometimes sure she might have took hold, her body would be quaking—uncontrollably. She closed her eyes. The older woman and the baby appeared. The older woman's house, which she had not seen, also appeared. She saw herself entering it. She saw herself showering with the older woman's soap and shampoo, drying off with fluffy towels. She saw herself snitching a swig of whatever the older woman kept to drink, saw herself kissing the baby all over his face. Then she saw herself fixing lunch: vegetable omelets and salad, bananas sliced into discs for the baby.

7.

When she fell asleep, she dreamed. Her mother, in a white bathrobe, a green towel around her head, stood in her kitchen, the way it'd been before they remodeled, smoking a cigarette. She did not say that she was sick or that she was going to have to die again, yet the younger woman could see this would happen: her mother had no hair. The younger woman tried to hug her, but her mother was deep in thought and did not respond.

8.

"I can't pay you right away," the older woman said.

"That's fine," the younger woman said. She'd not considered money.

The older woman led the younger woman through the rooms of the A-frame. She and her husband had built it ten years before with their very own hands. There were skylights and plants and wood floors and rugs. A white futon. A black recliner. A stereo. "These are his books," she said. "He loves to read. And these are his toys. Does he have enough? He doesn't like clothes but he understands a diaper is necessary."

The baby burbled. He beat his sippy cup against his chest. He blew milk bubbles.

"He's not ours," the older woman said, stooping down to peel a sticker off his foot. She wiped his mouth with her T-shirt. "I mean he's ours, but we didn't, you know, make him. We—I—can't. We looked for a long time. Then we were on this list—forever. They finally called us one night. They said they had someone, a boy. He was only two weeks old. But both his arms were broken. He wouldn't stop crying. He'd been thrown to the floor. When I first saw him, I cried. It was the only thing you could do. We took him home and for three weeks we were up all night every night with him." The older woman paused to squeeze his cheeks. "But you're fine now, aren't you? You're a big strong boy now, aren't you? Yes. Yes. That's my baby!"

9.

He was, the younger woman decided, a perfect baby. He came when you called him. He laughed when you squeezed his fat baby cheeks. He put the dead bug down when you said to. He did not eat the green booger on the tip of his finger but instead presented it to be taken away. He stayed very quiet when you read him *The Giving Tree*. He cooed quietly when you carried him around the living room, peering into drawers, opening cabinets, studying the books in the bookcase.

Though the younger woman found no books by the older woman, she counted ten books by the husband-poet. The books wanted her to think of the husband-poet as a rugged, untamed, unstable man. Each author photo was the same. In the photo he had a grizzled beard and wide eyes and a flannel shirt. Apparently, during ten books time, the husband's appearance had not changed.

"Will you take a nap?" she asked the baby. The baby smiled, lay down, and stuck his thumb in his mouth. The younger woman kissed him all over his face. She could eat him up, she said. He giggled, and fell asleep.

Outside it began to rain. The young woman chose a record—*Pink Moon*—and placed it on the turntable. She cracked eggs into a blue bowl. She tossed a salad with wooden tongs. It was good to cook. At the campsite, they had been living out of a leaky, stained cooler that a bear had recently smashed. The inside of the older woman's refrigerator gleamed white, and everything inside—imported cheese, wine, a jar of artichoke hearts, Greek olives, baby spinach, minced garlic, fresh cilantro—had come from far, far away.

"Jesus Christ!" the older woman screamed from the guest bedroom, which she now used as a studio. "Are you fucking crazy?" It took a moment for the younger woman to realize that the older woman was talking not to her but to her husband.

10.

"We can do this," the older woman said, stabbing a triangle of omelet and shutting her eyes. "We have this thing where we go away and go mad and return to each other." The younger woman nodded, as though she understood. "Forget it," the older woman said. "You. Tell me about your boyfriend."

"There's not much to tell," she said. Then the whole story poured out. The lifeguard. The party. The phone call. The accident.

The older woman lay down her fork and frowned. "What's his problem?"

"I know he's just being nice. I mean, he's nice to people."

The older woman shook her head. She said it sounded to her like the young woman could do better.

11.

When it was time to go the older woman offered to drive her. The younger woman said she could walk. "Oh," the older woman said, her eyes growing wide. She jogged to the tilting shed behind the A-frame and rolled out a bicycle. Cobwebs floated from the handlebars. It clattered and rattled and squeaked but it was still good. The younger woman took it. She rode it all the way back to the campsite, where she covered the bicycle with branches and leaves.

12.

"Uh, weren't we supposed to meet at the lake?" the boyfriend asked, as he got out of the van. A paper bag was bursting in his arms. He'd brought sausages and rice from the market.

"I got a ride," she said, dropping a load of branches she'd gathered onto the fire pit. He built a fire. She cooked. They drank beer and watched the fire die.

In the tent, when her boyfriend tried to reach into her sleeping bag, the younger woman scooched away. The boyfriend sighed. She asked how the lifeguard's boyfriend was and the boyfriend said, "Not so good." His truck had flipped four times. He would probably walk with a limp. The younger woman waited for her boyfriend to ask how her day had been, but he kept talking about the lifeguard and her boyfriend until she fell asleep, her calf twitching to the rhythms of his voice.

13.

Days passed. Each morning, after the boyfriend went to work, the younger woman uncovered the bicycle and rode to the A-frame. She ate breakfast with the older woman and the baby. She cleaned up after them. The mornings were spent with the baby while the older woman typed. At noon they all ate lunch together. Then the baby fell asleep on a blanket on the floor, and the two women drank coffee or smoked a joint or drank a beer. They talked. They held conversations. Sun streamed through the windows. Clouds descended and erased the trees. Rain lashed against the panes.

14.

It was hard sometimes not to stare at the older woman. The older woman could never be mistaken for a younger woman. In fact, there were too many lines in her face for her age. There were streaks in her hair and her teeth had grown yellow from cigarettes. Her body, however, had kept its shape. Her eyes, which bulged a little, had kept their blue. She was tall and slender and dark. She had soft-looking golden hairs on her legs. But the raw material of the older woman's body— while unforgettable—was not why the younger woman liked her. It was the way the younger woman heard herself speak, as if her real voice—the one she kept hidden—had given birth to itself.

15.

Sometimes the older woman wrote things down on scraps of paper, folded them up, and slid them into her pocket. When the younger woman told her that she was afraid she might have something inside her that would make her die, the older woman wrote this down on a subscription card for a magazine.

"See," the younger woman said.

"What?"

"My finger."

"Yes," the older woman said, taking it into her own. "You have nice hands. Do you play the piano?" She stroked the hand with her thumb.

"No, I mean *look*. It's twitching."

The woman shrugged. "Mine does that."

"You're making it do that."

"Whatever."

"Have you ever taken ecstasy?"

"I've taken plenty of other things." The older woman smiled.

16.

When the boyfriend found the bicycle, he asked what it was. "A bicycle," the younger woman said. He said he knew that, but what was it doing in the leaves and everything? She said she'd found it. The boyfriend was quiet. They looked for branches. He built a fire and cooked eggs. The younger woman, who was not hungry, refused to eat.

The boyfriend ate in silence. As he chewed, he placed his hand on the younger woman's leg. She moved her leg. He sighed.

"What?" she asked.

"Do you realize..." He clenched his jaw. "Never mind."

"What?"

"Can you even remember the last time we had sex?" He gestured with his fork. Egg flew into her lap.

"I don't keep track," the younger woman lied, flicking it away.

17.

That night, after a few beers, the younger woman allowed the boyfriend to go down on her. She tried to imagine the older woman. It was hard. The older woman would not have whiskers. The older woman would be gentle. The older woman would not be in a rush; she would not slide anything inside her. Afterward, the older woman would say something to make them laugh. That, and the older woman would sing.

18.

"Look!" the older woman called.

The younger woman ran into the studio. She watched a muscle spasm in the older woman's arm. The older woman smiled. The younger woman wondered if she was faking. She didn't care. She was entranced.

The phone rang. The older woman took the phone and left the room.

She had never been in the studio. The door was always

shut. A desk. A photo of a seacoast. Another of the baby. Another of the same picture of the husband-poet—the same that was inside his books. The younger woman considered the possibility that the husband-poet was a figment of the older woman's imagination. She looked at the computer screen. There was nothing there. A cursor blinked, a lone stripe bobbing in the whiteness.

19.

"One of his fucking students," the older woman whispered. "Young enough to be his daughter," she said.

"Oh my God," the younger woman said. She tried to act surprised.

"It's okay," the older woman said, sipping from a glass of tremulous water.

"Would you mind watching the baby?" the older woman asked. The younger woman said of course. She didn't ask why the older woman didn't stay right here so she could take care of her. The older woman took off all her clothes and stood in front of her closet. The younger woman tried not to stare. "That looks good," she said, when the older woman held up a blouse and pants, and the older woman put them on. She grabbed her keys and some lipstick, and ran out the door.

When the older woman's Jeep lurched out of sight, the baby began to cry.

20.

When the older woman returned, it was dark. The baby was asleep. "I had some drinks," the older woman said, slinging her keys into the couch. "They didn't do a fucking thing." She lit a cigarette, took a drag, placed it in the sink. She wobbled.

"Who did you see?" the younger woman asked.

"An old friend," she said, lighting another cigarette. The younger woman sensed this was a lie—perhaps she had simply gone to a bar and asked for a bottle.

The older woman grabbed the younger woman by the arm. She had something to tell her, she said, something *important*: she'd seen the lifeguard and the boyfriend together. When she left the bar, she'd taken a walk. They were down by the lake, on the swings.

The younger woman frowned.

"It's true," the older woman said, releasing the younger woman's arm and taking a drag on her cigarette. The lifeguard, she said, had unbuttoned her shirt. The older woman exhaled a plume of smoke, and described what had happened. She described it with a smile.

The younger woman laughed. She laughed because it could not be true. She laughed because the older woman was laughing.

"I'm sorry," the older woman said, kneeling before the younger woman. Then she threw up.

21.

The younger woman cleaned the older woman's face. She helped her out of her clothes. She washed the older woman's vomit from their hands and put her to bed. Then she lay down beside her in the sheets she had changed earlier that morning, and tried not to think about her boyfriend or the lifeguard. She was here now with the older woman, who obviously needed her help. After the older woman closed her eyes, after she began to breathe deeply, the younger woman pressed her nose against the older woman's neck. The fragrance annihilated every other smell and filled up her head. The older woman woke and kneaded the back of the younger woman's neck with her hands. The younger woman cried a little, then fell asleep in the arms of the older woman, who whispered into her ear and stroked her hair.

22.

The younger woman dreamed of her mother. As in previous dreams where she'd come back to life, though she'd become sick again, she refused to hug. Instead, she lit a cigarette. "This place is a wreck," she said, and flip-flopped away.

23.

When the younger woman woke, her arms were wrapped around the older woman, their bodies two spoons. She did not move. She was aware of pulsations—her own heartbeat. Her lips were pressed against the older woman's ear, and she feared her breathing might wake her. She touched her tongue to her ear. She moved it slowly. The older woman flinched. The younger woman closed her eyes.

24.

The younger woman was by herself, at the campsite, trying to take off her clothes. Sweaters, socks, boots, long underwear, pants—layers and layers. Her boyfriend drove up in the van. The younger woman asked the boyfriend where he had been. He said, "Looking for you."

He hugged her. She wanted to ask about the lifeguard but she knew if she asked she would cry. She would cry because he had once been her best friend and now he might have forgotten her. She realized that she was hugging the lifeguard, who wore only her bathing suit. The lifeguard blew her whistle at the younger woman.

25.

The younger woman woke. She was alone in the bed.

The older woman was folding clothes and laying them inside a suitcase. "I'm going to find him," she said. "And when I do he will know."

"Know what?"

"He'll just know."

As the younger woman helped her pack, the older woman said nothing of the previous night. Perhaps nothing had happened. They spent the rest of the day placing things into boxes and bags and suitcases and tying knots with rope and filling up the Jeep. The older woman had the radio on as they worked. When the older woman wasn't looking, the younger woman sneaked some things that didn't belong to her into her backpack: a roll of undeveloped film, the T-shirt the older woman had slept in, and a page of the older woman's manuscript she'd thrown into the trash.

The roll of film, once developed, would be blank. The manuscript page, unfolded, would contain a partially decipherable description of a dream the younger woman had dreamed. The T-shirt, unwadded, would be mashed against her face—a filter, sometimes, through which she would breathe.

26.

It took most of the day to pack the Jeep. When they were finished, the older woman announced she was taking the younger woman out to dinner. As they drove to the restaurant, they passed the younger woman's boyfriend. He was alone. He was driving fast. He squinted through the glass, his ashen face hovering over the wheel. The younger woman wondered whether he was looking for her.

At a lakefront restaurant, a moose head watched them eat. The younger woman told herself it might be a scene from the future. This is what the future would look like if they lived in the mountains at the edge of a lake. Once a week they would go out to eat, where they would sit, like this, in the dim lamplight and stare at each other. They would love each other and they wouldn't care who saw them. They would, as they did now, take turns feeding the baby. They would laugh, as they did now, when the baby slung spaghetti, when a broccoli floret tumbled into the younger woman's lap.

The older woman reached across the table. She touched the younger woman's hand. She grasped it. She smiled. Rings gleamed on her fingers. A bracelet glinted in the light. She did not say, "I love you" or "I will miss you." She did not say, "You can't stay here! You're coming with me." She did not say, "We could take care of one another, and of the baby, who, now that he's been abandoned by two fathers, is ours."

She said, "You've been so good to us." When the younger woman's mouth trembled, the older woman smiled. "We'll write," she said. "We'll stay in touch."

27.

Diving. Diving. Diving. Diving. It was as if the younger woman didn't know anything about the older woman until she saw her diving in the river that ran beside the place where they'd eaten. Plunging underwater, holding her breath, looking for the keys—it was simply another task that had to be completed before she left. The younger woman could see, though, that she'd already gone. Already, she was driving to-ward the husband-poet, refusing to acknowledge the possibility that he might not even exist.

Even after it was too dark to see, the older woman—slippery, goose-pimpled, drowning—refused to give up. The younger woman decided she would wait, patiently, until the older woman came to her senses. She would wait until she crawled out of the stream: shivering, hair tangled, skin blue with cold. The younger woman would go find a towel, but then she would not know what to do. As she waited, the younger woman told herself everything was fine. The keys were sleeping peacefully underwater. Her boyfriend was somewhere, driving, running, yelling out her name, looking for her. The baby, his head against her shoulder, cooed in her arms. Muscles all over her body were twitching—something dark, something light, trying to burst through, trying, without success, to open her up. As the river kept running, kept pouring more of itself into itself, the younger woman, who could see the blur of the older woman's body beneath the surface, the whiteness of her arms as she searched among the rocks, began to count. She didn't know what she was counting, but she knew she wanted numbers. She liked the way they led so naturally from one to the other, the way they appeared to give order. She liked the feel of them in her mouth as she whispered them—a secret—into the baby's ear. As the older woman surfaced and, growing weary, went under again.

THE DIGGING

They call it free labor. When you've broken enough rules at Wildwood Adventist Academy, it's what you get. You wake before dawn and after a breakfast of powdered eggs, applesauce, toast, and meatless meat, you follow Principal Hedrick down Freshman Hall, out the emergency exit, past the gymnasium—empty at this hour except for Mr. Wolff, who's unfolding gym mats for circuit training—and into a field next to the industrial arts building, where you begin your gloveless shoveling until the hole is waist deep and as long as your body. When you're done? Fill it back up.

Kyle doesn't mind the digging. The blade *schlucking* into the ground, his flesh quivering as he hoists slabs of pink clay from the hole—that's fine. He can deal with the heat, too, as long as he takes pulls from the jug of piss-warm water at the edge of the hole. Even the damp T-shirt is tolerable, despite the fact that its cracked *Metallica* iron-on—turned chestwards so as not to exert a bad influence upon his fellow students—is chafing his left nipple.

It's the letter that bothers him—the letter, folded this morning into the back pocket of his jeans, that he can't stop thinking about, even though recalling particular lines is not unlike shooting himself in the chest, the words scattering through his body like bird shot. The letter—which traveled two hundred miles, from the loft of an A-frame in the Blue Ridge Mountains to Kyle's mail slot at the dorm—was penned by a girl named Raven, a girl with purple streaks in her hair, a silver bead she inserts into the side of her nose as soon as school's out, and a sketchbook of the tattoos she plans to ink into her back once she turns eighteen. Raven is—

or was, since after what's happened he doesn't know if the term can still be applied—Kyle's girlfriend, and according to the letter, she's seriously distressed. So distressed, in fact, that she wasn't able to say what Kyle believes she really wanted to say, which was, "Come home." Which is exactly what Kyle's wanted to do ever since his mother and Jake Tucker delivered him to the hot flat heart of Georgia and left him there to live at a school for people who believe that Saturday is the Sabbath of the Lord thy God.

At the academy, it's three strikes and you're out, which means, technically, Kyle should've already got the boot. The administration, however, decided to give him a break. Principal Hedrick—stroking his knit tie, bearing squarish teeth with spaces in between—said he'd never lost a parent, but he acknowledged it had to be hard, especially the way Kyle's father had gone. He said he understood it could be hard to fit in at a new place and that if you lost sight of the reason you were here—i.e., to nurture a Christlike spirit—a boarding school might seem overly concerned with rules. Believe it or not, he said, before he got rebaptized, he used to be a rule breaker, too. He'd had the long hair. He'd worn the t-shirts with double meanings, experimented with tobacco products. Kyle, he'd said, reminded him of himself. He knew that underneath whatever was making Kyle do the things he'd done, Kyle had a good heart. So after prayerful consideration, Hedrick and Vice Principal Stokes and Dean Reich had decided they would make an exception: they'd give Kyle another chance.

Now, instead of expulsion, Kyle's digging a hole—a punishment that has its benefits, considering he's been able to skip chapel and classes. A couple times, he's even lost himself in the digging, but only momentarily: lines from Raven's letter—*We just kind of started doing things; please don't hurt him*—keep flying through his head. Plus, it's impossible to dig a man-sized hole without thinking *grave*, and thus without seeing his father's coffin, like some glossy wooden missile, its little window flipped open so people could walk by and say, "They shore done a good job on 'im." Granted, it'd been amazing that the funeral director could've made a face with what had been left over, but the face wore an expression the man had never used, an expression which made it look like despite being dead he was troubled, that maybe he could see, through his eyelids, the people passing by—as though somewhere in his dead body he was still alive.

Kyle can't shake the feeling that, any minute, his shovel will strike something solid, that the rusted blade will make a divot in some half-rotten, long-forgotten pine box, the kind his granny has already commissioned a man to build back home, a box made from a pine felled behind her house, a box she has crawled into and said, "Yes, that's it, that's exactly how I want it to feel, no frills, just me in this box with no formaldehyde in my veins, just me and this box returning to dust, to be called up when the Lord comes to take us home."

So when the tip of Kyle's blade hits something hard, he drops the shovel and kneels. Turns out it's only a wedge of slate, but when he lifts it up, a millipede wriggles out. Kyle jumps back; the rock splats against the dirt. There are some things he doesn't mind—he'll grab a copperhead by the tail and sling it through the woods—but he can't stand bugs.

Last May, four months after Kyle's father's funeral, insects invaded the house where Kyle had grown up: tiny, armored ovals that scurried into shadows, away from the light. Kyle spent hours going through the house with a box of

Kleenex, and each time he snapped a bug body inside the tissue, he shuddered. Eventually, Kyle's mother summoned an exterminator—a tall, heavy-lidded man with a deep voice and a dark tan that made Kyle wonder if he had Indian blood—who, after he'd squirted the nooks and crannies of the house with poison, accepted a sweet tea from Kyle's mother. On the way out, Jake Tucker handed her a leaflet bearing the beasts of Revelation, his number scribbled beneath a tusked bear.

By June—after a series of Bible studies with Jake Tucker at the table where Kyle's father used to clean his guns—a robed pastor lowered Kyle's mother into a mountain stream, thus officially uniting her to the body of the Seventh-day Adventist Church, whose members believed the Bible was a road map to be interpreted by the Spirit of Prophecy, made manifest within a young prophetess named Ellen Gould White, a woman whose visions told people how to live: don't drink, don't smoke, don't drink caffeinated beverages, don't swear, don't gamble, don't touch yourself, don't consult mediums or talk to ghosts (because the dead are dead and ghosts are demons in disguise), don't eat flesh foods (they arouse animal passions), don't visit the cinema (your angel won't follow you inside), love not the world and its diversions, guard the edges of the Sabbath, commune constantly with Christ, and watch out for Satan, who lies always in wait and knows your every weakness.

By mid-July, Kyle's mother was engaged, but since Jake Tucker believed jewelry was an adornment of the heathen, she wore no ring. The couple delivered the news to Kyle one Saturday night at the Western Sizzlin. Kyle's mother smiled brightly and squeezed Kyle's hand with her cold, bony fingers; Jake Tucker, stuffing slabs of butter into a steaming perforation in his baked potato, said he knew he could never take the place of Kyle's daddy but that he loved Kyle's mother very much and that he already thought of Kyle like a son, had even convinced members of the Valleytown S.D.A. Church to consider Kyle a worthy student, so that once fall arrived, he could attend a boarding academy like other Adventist kids. Kyle gave an appreciative nod, then excused himself, and on his way to the bathroom, where he punched a paper-towel dispenser and let himself cry into a wad of sandpapery tissue, he couldn't help but imagine his father—orange Husqvarna hat, camouflage rain jacket—hovering over the salad bar, spit-shining the sneeze guards, loading up on the garbanzos, and shaking his head because he couldn't believe that this Jake guy—this quasi-evangelist-bug-man—would soon be sleeping in his bed.

The slab of slate is nearly the size of Kyle's torso, and heavy. He decides—just to get it out of the way—to haul it into the woods. It's a ways off—fifty yards, maybe—but the work of transporting an unwieldy burden feels good: with each step, Kyle puffs air out of his mouth, like his father used to do when he bear-hugged two-hundred-pound logs and toted them to the homemade wood splitter, a machine whose blade, powered by a hydraulic pump, could slice through the heart of the toughest oak.

When Kyle feels the rock slipping from his hands, he starts to waddle-jog, and once he reaches the trees he hurls the rock forward, where it barely clears his feet. He squats to rest, peering into the scraggly loblollies—the kind of pines loggers plant back home after they've clear-cut. He hopes for a glimpse of something wild—a deer or a turkey or a grouse—but there's nothing, not even a squirrel; the forest is dead. The uniformity of these woods, their identical rows of pines, it's a bad dream of what woods should be. Unlike the mountains, where a new kind of foliage blooms at every turn and each hemlock and rhododendron thicket becomes a kind of landmark, you'd get lost easy here.

"The kids look happy," his mother said, examining the glossy academy brochures, which arrived only a few days after Jake Tucker suggested Kyle go. The house was silent except for the new clock Jake had placed on the mantel—a miniature grandfather with a loud, insistent tick like the timer on a bomb. Kyle's mother was smiling at the pictures: boys and girls dribbling basketballs, boys and girls flashing peace signs, boys and girls wearing bathrobes, reenacting something biblical. The thing was, Kyle's mother had never been much of a smiler. Kyle's mother had worked for fifteen years at the Lee plant in Valleytown, sewing jeans under fluorescent lights, enveloped in the eternal thunder of a hundred machines and the voices shouting above them. Each night, when she'd come home, she'd made Hamburger Helper and green bean casseroles, folded clothes while watching taped episodes of *Guiding Light*. But she rarely smiled. She didn't smile whenever Kyle and his father let big ones at the dinner table. She didn't smile when Kyle and his father wrestled in the living room or announced their return from a successful hunt with hound-dog whoops. Now, though, eight months after his father's death, it was as if his mother were making up for lost time: the Good News—the *seventh* day is the Sabbath, there is no eternal hellfire, the dead are asleep until Jesus comes—lit up her face.

As Kyle studied the brochures, part of him longed to escape into the bizarre, parentless world of academy kids, even if it did mean attending chapel and working four hours a day as a janitor or a groundskeeper or a dishwasher or an assembler of carpet sample books at a factory on the edge of campus. But Kyle didn't want to leave Raven, a quasi-Goth girl whose parents—a couple of hippies who owned a white-water-rafting business—had finally allowed her to abandon home school and transfer to Nantahala High, a girl who'd befriended Kyle after he'd delivered a paper last January in Social Science class about the inability of federal agents to find Eric Rudolph, a man the government claimed had set off a bomb during the 1996 Olympics in Atlanta, then abandoned his truck at a nearby campground and disappeared into the mountains where they lived. "If you ever want to go look for him," Raven said, slipping Kyle a strip of black paper with her number written in silver, "let me know."

That spring, while leashed bloodhounds tugged men in fatigues and bullet proof vests through rhododendron thickets, Kyle and Raven rode Kyle's ATV up an old logging road, crashing through creek beds and over fallen logs, leaves licking their arms and faces as they neared the lot at the top of the mountain where a house—which Kyle's father had helped build for a rich doctor from Atlanta—had burned down. They'd sit on a concrete slab and crush chunks of ash with their shoes, and talk about whether or not the BVDs they'd found in the rubble belonged to the fugitive, about what they would do if they were on the run. A couple of times, Raven brought up Kyle's father, and Kyle said he'd rather not talk about it, which was a lie—he just didn't want her to see him cry. At some point, Raven would flip open a compact mirror, revealing a joint she'd rolled from her parents' stash, the weed crackling once she held a match, struck against her zipper, to the wilted tip.

Once, Kyle's friend, Hal Tatham—a tall, gangly boy with a shaved head—came along, and they boosted their highs with warm beer he'd scored from a cousin's convenience mart, tossing empties into the rich doctor's kidney-shaped pool that'd turned green. Later, when it was just Kyle and Raven, they retrieved some of the floaters and set them against what was left of the chimney, and Kyle taught her how to aim and fire the .22 pistol he'd managed to swipe from his father's cabinet before his mother had the chance to pawn it, whispering, "that's good" and "hold it still," inhaling the smell of gunpowder and of her neck, which was tangy with sweat, and which, once his had lips grazed, he began to kiss. Eventually, he made his way to her mouth. The gun tumbled into the rubble, and his hands snaked, thanks to her directions, into her jeans.

Kyle can feel the letter crinkle in his back pocket every time he bends over, every time he raises his right leg or jams the shovel into the soil. Maybe, he thinks, the perspiration pouring from his body will bleed through his jeans to the letter, blurring Raven's words, thus revising the message, transforming it into the kind of dispatch Raven used to send: that which pledged her eternal love. For a second, Kyle convinces himself a mutation of this sort is possible, and wants to check, to yank out the letter and read it again, but then he hears an alarm in the distance, a series of electric bleats, and thinks maybe someone has pulled another fire alarm. Turns out it's just Dean Reich opening one of the emergency exits of the boy's dorm. The mustachioed man-blob that is Reich stands there for a moment, watching Kyle, monitoring him. Once satisfied, he returns to the bowels of the dorm, and in his mind Kyle can see him traveling along the bleach-stained carpet, his ears, like a dog's, listening for the slightest beat, the slightest tinny jangle, a signal announcing the presence of a boy with a Walkman, contraband Reich will gleefully confiscate.

Why no one else had thought of pulling the fire alarms—and why the repeated alarm-pulling never inspired others to join the rebellion—is still a mystery to Kyle: after all, Wildwood Academy has structured itself in such a way that disruption seems the only adequate response. From meal-times (where meatless breakfast links or meatless meat loaf or meatless burger patties bubble in aluminum trays) to morning chapel (where you gather with other students to sing songs about panting deer and the blood of the Lamb) to classes (where last week, in health, Ms. Bose clicked through slides of lesioned penises and blistered vaginas to illustrate what sex outside of marriage could do) to work detail (where if you're a janitor, you might peel tampons from bathroom tiles, replace urinal cakes, or bring a bottle of industrial chemicals to your nose until it erases every thought in your head) to rec period (an hour of free time when, if you can't play basketball or practice gymnastics on the stage of the gym or flip skateboards onto the concrete benches outside, you lose consecutive games of foosball to a guy named Ben Schlarb) to evening chapel (where boys gather in the room above the dean's apartment, the smell of their farts and sweat filling the room like some kind of Incense of the Damned) to study hall (where, locked in your room for three hours, you scribble letters that pledge you will soon come home for good) to lights out (at ten-thirty, when the power to your room is shut off), Wildwood Adventist Academy ensures that every hour of every day has a purpose and that every student is accounted for.

The first time the alarms blared and students filed out of the administration building, Kyle could tell his classmates were grateful for the disruption, and they might've even thanked him for getting them out of the test or quiz or Bible sword drill had they known it was him, which they didn't, not until Hedrick caught him—hiding in a bathroom stall after the third false alarm in a week—and then they rolled their eyes and shook their heads as though the stunt was unfathomably lame.

Alarm pulling had been the first strike; Kyle was roombound for a week.

The second strike came three days later when, after study hall, the chapel bells rang and the boys began to make their way upstairs, some dragging blankets and pillows, some toting textbooks, some shirtless, some robed, some fully dressed in school attire: slacks and button-up shirts. Finally, Dean Reich—attempting to hide his burgeoning man boobs inside a baggy Falcons jersey—arrived. He wanted to know who'd lifted the 24-pack of grape soda and the case of Mars bars from the dorm store. Nobody confessed, so they sat there until midnight while Reich and the hall monitors searched the rooms.

Kyle never knew whether they recovered the candy and soda, or what they'd found in anyone else's room, but he knew what they found in his, because the next day he was summoned to the Dean's Office, where Reich produced a shoe box. "This yours?" Reich asked, shaking the box, as if the way the things rattled inside offered a verdict. He removed the dented lid, revealing a can of Skoal, a ten-inch hunting knife, and a slightly warped cassette: Metallica, *Master of Puppets*. Reich wanted to know why Kyle had brought these things to a Christian School and what he planned to do with them. If Reich hadn't been such an asshole, Kyle might have explained (those were the things he'd taken from the glove box of his dead father's truck), but the last thing he wanted from the fat fuck was sympathy, so he kept his mouth shut and massaged his temples, pretending to think, when really he was composing a letter to Raven about the absurdity of the situation, how the funny thing was that his father might've got a kick out of it, and how Raven didn't know how good she had it, even if she did have to milk goats and eat her mom's lima bean curry while her dad praised the fidelity of his latest live Dead bootleg—a reverie Reich interrupted by crushing the Metallica cassette with his fist, wrapping the tape ribbon around the Skoal and the knife and tossing the whole knotted caboodle into the trash.

Dirt flies. Kyle plunges the shovel into the dirt, flings the dirt into the air, squints as the dirt particles rain down upon him. He digs faster. Harder. He tells himself he's digging a hole not through earth, but through some kind of flesh, through the membrane of time itself, tunneling back to last autumn, back in the pre-Raven days when his father was alive, when Kyle and Hal Tatham were still friends, when they fished together, watched late-night soft-core on Showtime, drove Hal's dad's police cruiser to Valleytown and back, flipping on the siren a couple of times even though they promised they wouldn't.

The unfair thing? None of that will happen again. Now it's just him and this hole and, when he goes back to the dorm, eighty-two obnoxious Adventist boys—Koreans slurping stinky noodles from hot pots, blacks bumping each other's fists as they jog down the halls, skaters rolling D&D dice when Reich's not looking. Once Kyle reaches his room, he'll crawl into a sleeping bag and rest his head upon an an-

MATTHEW VOLLMER

archy sign some previous sleeper tattooed across the sticky
mattress flesh and reread the letter and wish he is dead, not
because he wants to die, but because that's the only way he'll
be able to stop the hole in his chest from growing larger, a
yawning mouth threatening to suck him inside out. Then it'll
be him and his roommate, Ben Schlarb, a poor kid in a tropical shirt, crotch-high shorts, church socks, and a pair of
battered sneakers, his hair parted with some kind of pomade.
Just Kyle and Schlarb and Schlarb's mouth, orbited by oozing
acne, which will yap about his missionary days in Nairobi,
and about how African women love sex and that all you have
to do is show them the sign, all you have to do is raise your
balled fist in the air, which means, according to Schlarb, let's
go into the bushes. The sad thing, the thing that gets Kyle
every time, is that he never has the heart to tell Schlarb to
shut up.

Kyle's hands—slipping against the shovel—burn. Blis-
ters, he knows, are inevitable. He lifts his head from the hole,
blinks, nearly blacks out. Once his vision rights, he sees a host
of freshmen boys exiting the gym, where, no doubt, Mr. Wolf,
making fart sounds with his hands, has cheered them
through circuit training while "Eye of the Tiger," the only officially sanctioned rock song Kyle is aware of, blasted through
blown-out speakers. Some of the boys notice Kyle and yell.
Some keep their heads down. Some pop each other in the
nuts. Only one of them actually screams Kyle's name, and
that's Schlarb, who flips Kyle a discreet bird, grins, then disappears into the industrial arts building, to varnish the
creepers the boys have made for their fathers to slide beneath
the vehicles they drive, primitive machines the fathers will
receive graciously and then discard.

Kyle drops the shovel, swabs his brow. He lets a string of

spit drip from the tip of his lip to the ground, nudges a clod into the hole with his boot.

"Not tired yet, are you?"

Kyle whips around. Behind him: a short, stout man with bearish arms. A man in a plaid shirt, creased slacks, and pointy shoes. *Hedrick.*

"Lunchtime," Hedrick says, sliding his Ray Bans into his tufty gray hair and turning down the lip of a McDonald's bag. "Don't tell anyone this came from me," he adds, winking. *God*, Kyle thinks, *that's so Hedrick.* Bending the rules ever so slightly, as if he understands your need for what you aren't supposed to have, when really, all he wants is adoration or, at the least, leverage, so that if you fuck up later, he can say that you shit on him.

"It's here when you need it." Hedrick sets the bag on the ground. He salutes. "Carry on," he says, jogging away, the hundred keys ringed to his belt jingling.

Once Hedrick's far enough away, Kyle unfolds the bag, flicks pickles off the patties, wolfs down the lukewarm burgers. Despite the fact that he wants to think Hedrick's a dick, he's thankful for the meat. Each majestically cheesy bite obliterates his taste buds, reminds him of post Little League Happy Meals when, after the Nantahala Hawks got squashed by whoever they were playing, Kyle and his father would drive to the nearest McDonald's gorge themselves on burgers, fries, apple pies.

"I like to come up here to think," his father said, last fall, during Kyle's first trip to the burned-down house. They'd parked beside the garage—the fire hadn't touched it—and from the cab they had a great view of the ruins and the valley below. "I look at what's left of this house and think about how perfect it was, how that doctor wanted everything *just* right. And by God, it was. Son, they had everything. Big ol' fireplace… Jacuzzi tubs… bar. Big-screen TV. Everything. But then a wire caught fire inside. Whole thing went down in an hour. Just that quick, and poof. Everything gone."

Eventually, he leaned forward, pulled a piece of notebook paper from his back pocket and spread it out on his thigh. Kyle recognized the paper immediately—the sketches filling the page were his: a fanged woman sucking blood from another woman's neck, a samurai falling upon his sword, a bucktoothed boy chainsawing his leg off.

The page trembled in his father's hand. "I," he began. "I guess I just want you to know that it's okay to feel things you think you might not ought to feel." Kyle nodded. The rest of his body was paralyzed. His father had never talked like this before; his voice warbled. "You can't help," his father continued, "what you feel. I think it's important for you to know that. My daddy, he never told me that. I wished he would've. I wished he would've said it was okay sometimes to be sad. To think about this kind of stuff. Me, I don't see anything wrong with it." He waggled the page. "I see it as you gettin' out whatever you need to get out. But your mother… she don't see it that way. All I'm sayin' is be careful what you leave out. What you let her find."

Kyle wanted to tell his father that the drawings didn't mean anything. That the vampire women had come from one of Hal's comic books; that he'd drawn the samurai because Mr. Young had mentioned hara-kiri in history class; and that he'd drawn the man sawing his leg off because he'd been thinking about how Rudolph's brother had sliced off his hand with a band saw to protest the search. Kyle wanted to tell his father that he wasn't sad, that he didn't really think about this kind of stuff, but he didn't, he just nodded again, and they sat there, staring through a windshield splattered with bugs. Finally, Kyle's father said, "Well, I just wanted to talk a little while with you," and Kyle said, "Okay," and they drove away.

At the far end of the campus, which Kyle has to squint to see, kids are lining up at the door of the blue bus for the weekly town trip. During last week's trip, Kyle planned to use the Wal-Mart pay phone to call in a bomb threat—an idea Hal had written in the margin of one of Raven's letters. *In the spirit of Rudolph*, Hal had scribbled, and Kyle had chuckled, because a bomb threat was so Hal, so overdone—though Kyle couldn't think of anyplace that deserved one more than Wildwood Adventist Academy. To prepare himself, he sucked down three suicides at the free refill station at Taco Bell, then ambled across the Wal-Mart parking lot to a pay phone, only to find he'd shoved the remainder of his change into the wrong pocket, the one with the hole.

"So stupid," he whispers, crushing a dirt clod beneath his boot. His father—an accomplished practical joker—would've never fumbled a prank like that. The week before his father's death, they came down the mountain, into Valleytown, and parked the truck in front of Ingles grocery, next to a news van with its satellite dish aimed heavenward. There, cameramen used the mountains as backdrop and reporters said things like "Rudolph is still at large" and "These mountains are impenetrable." The reporters were ridiculous, what with their grave faces whose expressions involved only the raising and lowering of their eyebrows and whose eyes couldn't stop blinking. Beneath a sign advertising beef tips for ninety-nine cents a pound, Kyle's father spat his teeth into his Big Gulp cup and inserted a pinch of Skoal into his mouth, forcing—as he winked at Kyle—a string of brown drool down his chin. Moments later, a guy holding a Fox mic appeared and asked Kyle's father—whose Dale Earnhardt T-shirt was conveniently still covered in sawdust and whose toothless face had a four-month beard going—if he would like to be interviewed. Kyle's father frowned. "Dang," he said, "you mean awwn TayVee?" The reporter said maybe and Kyle's father said sure, and when the reporter asked Kyle's father what his name was, his father pulled Lonnie P. Cacklepuss out of his ass, which nearly caused Kyle to blow Mountain Dew out of his nose. And when the reporter asked, "Mr. Cacklepuss, would you hide Rudolph?," Kyle's father said, "Why not? Hell, if he showed up on my stoop, I'd give ol' Rudolph some pork rinds and a foot massage," which was funny but also true, because Kyle's father took all people in, no matter what their hurt or what they'd done, that's how he is. Was.

The hole is waist deep now, and Kyle steps inside. He squats. He reclines. He mashes the back of his head against the dirt. Then he slips the pages from his back pocket, takes a deep breath, and dives in:

Dear Kyle,

I came home from school today, totally bummed because Mrs. Greer's gave us this research paper to write, and I have no idea whatsoever what to write about. So (naturally) I roll up a joint, and I'm listening to the new Wu-Tang record and thinking you would so hate it, because this is like totally the opposite of all that metal stuff you like, and before I know it, like, a whole hour has passed. Well, I guess I left the roach in the living room ashtray, and when Mom found it there, she totally freaked out, saying what if somebody saw it there, what if the FBI came by like they did the other day, just to check to see if we'd heard anything about Rudolph (like there's anything to hear) and what if their dogs had like smelled it or something? At which point I had this vision of them taking my parents away, just for a little while, so I could have the house to myself, and I wouldn't have to listen to the Dead or watch them do yoga together or clean out the Jacuzzi, and touch those dead lizards at the bottom that dissolve in your hands and make you want to barf. Speaking of barfing, I guess I have something to tell you, something that will probably freak you out, maybe even make you sick, because Kyle I swear it has totally made me sick, and I wish I could just bottle it up and never have to show it to you, but I'm going to anyway. So here goes. Remember me telling you how some of us rode in the bus to watch Nantahala play Murphy last week? And how Hal fired the winning shot with like no time on the clock? Well, actually, there was this other part I forgot to tell you, which was that on the way back, it was dark and everyone was cheering and I really had no idea how it happened, maybe it had something to do with the dark and the fact that Hal was wearing the same kind of Speed Stick you use, but one minute I was giving Hal a congratulatory hug, and the next minute, well, we just kind of started doing things, and even though I knew it was wrong, I kept going, because honestly, it just felt so good to touch someone else, it was like all this loneliness just went away, like I was on fire again, like with you, like before, and when we got back to the school parking lot, Hal gave me a ride, where we kind of did even more things to each other. I don't expect you to understand, but please, please don't hurt Hal, it wasn't his fault, it was mine. If you're going to hurt anyone, hurt me.

Hurt him Kyle thought, the first time he read the letter, the day before, in his dorm room, while Ben Schlarb knelt on the floor, gazing out the window, hoping someone in the girl's dorm would flash him. *Hurt him* didn't come close to describing what Kyle had planned for Hal Tatham. His pulse quickened—a panicky beat whose power begged to be harnessed. He could feel the anger swelling in his chest, his arms, his legs, and he longed for the sweet sting of his knuckles smashing the bridge of Hal's nose, the crunch of a boot cracking ribs. At that moment, Win Bradke, a mulleted redhead from North Dakota, waltzed into the room. Win Bradke was bored, wanted to show off, wanted to dominate someone, wanted attention, wanted laughs, wanted who knows what, and these nameless desires compelled him to scan the room for something to manhandle. Finally, he plucked Ben Schlarb's retainer from the edge of the sink and, as though admiring some precious jewel, hoisted it into the light. After an approving nod, and despite Schlarb's pathetic "Please don't," Win slid the retainer down the front of his pants, vigorously rubbing it against his pubes. Once relieved of his itch, Win Bradke returned the retainer ever so gently to the edge of the sink. That's when Kyle leaped up and kicked Win as hard as he could in the nuts, and when the big North Dakotan hit the floor, Kyle started in on his face.

It feels good to take a load off, to wallow in the sticky dirt. As long as Kyle's down in the hole, nobody can see him, which is nice, because here at Wildwood Adventist Academy, privacy is almost impossible to come by. Everywhere you go, there's someone monitoring you, some manatee-shaped man or woman pumped up on soy-meat nitrates observing you with a suspicious eye because you can't be trusted, not even for a second, you might fondle someone, you might fondle yourself, you might make an obscene gesture, you might attempt an escape. Until now, Kyle hasn't found a place guaranteeing solitude—even that old standby, the bathroom, has failed him. You can't reflect in the shower, because it's you and five other guys gathered at six a.m. around a steel pole, out of which protrude six nozzles, and when you're lathering up, sometimes you nudge your neighbor's love handles, bump rumps. Even when taking a shit, you usually have to see the next person's shoes in the next stall over, have to inhale, if not through your nose, then your mouth, the exhalations of your fellow man.

Here, though, in the hole, the only person who can see Kyle—assuming He's actually watching—is the Almighty, and Kyle considers launching a prayer beyond the cumuli, but when he closes his eyes, he's back in his old house, where he hears the shot again, a pop like a firecracker. Then he's wandering out the back door, across the half-frozen yard and into the shed, where fleshy chunks of turf dangle from the blades of go-devils and shovels on the walls, where old gas cans and toolboxes and bike pumps make walking precarious, and where, when Kyle spots his father slumped against the riding mower, he knows he's seeing something that no son should ever have to see, but he can't stop looking, because while these are his father's arms and his father's hands and legs and boots and hair, this is not his father's face. His father's face has a nose and eyes and mouth and beard. This face is not a face at all. It is a mess. It is blood and pulp and tissue. And because it is so incomprehensible, Kyle lingers, waiting for his father to get up, to pull off the ingenious disguise, to sling the face that is not his face at Kyle, and say, "I got you."

It isn't the first time that Kyle has whispered the words, "Your father is dead" or "Your father is gone and you can't bring him back," but it is the first time since he's been at Wildwood that he hasn't had to get ahold of himself because he was waiting in a cafeteria line or reciting intransitive Spanish verbs or listening to a guest speaker endorse, with ingratiating earnestness, the power of prayer—the first time since he arrived two months ago that he's been able to adequately torture himself with the realization that he will never again wrap his arms around his father's bulk, never again inhale the gasoline and sawdust and Copenhagen wafting from his body, never again watch the man lay a fire with old newspaper and kindling or hoist a trout out of the water with his bare hands or tug the beard he could never remember to trim.

It begins then, silently: Kyle's mouth stretching wide, his chest convulsing soundlessly. Then it hits and Kyle is gone, disappearing into the storm that is his grief.

When Kyle opens his eyes, he realizes that he must've blacked out for a second—must've fallen into a brief, dreamless sleep. He rises to a sitting position, presses the pages of the letter to his chest, and shudders. It's bright—the afternoon sun casting light into the hole—and the skin of his arms and face feels burned. That's when he notices Hedrick standing above him, hands on his hips, Ray-Bans on his forehead, tie flapping in the wind. "For a minute there," Hedrick says, grinning and shaking his head, "I thought you were dead." Then Hedrick, being Hedrick, does something ridiculous. Something uncalled for. He climbs into the hole.

"Nice place," he says, sitting down Indian-style.

God, Kyle thinks, wiping his nose on the back of his

hand, *the man has no shame.* He slides a fingernail under a clump of dirt at the edge of his boots, somewhat angry that he allowed himself to break down like he did, ashamed that Hedrick might've heard him bawling like a baby. Hedrick asks him what he's reading and Kyle squints back at him, and when he sees Hedrick's face—the beady eyes, the slight smirk, the gray five o'clock shadow—he wants to tell him everything, to shock this Goody Two-shoes with a profanity-fueled description of his father's fatal self-inflicted wound or a play-by-play of the unsavory utterances his mother and Jake Tucker produced one night behind the closed door of the master bedroom or accounts of ganja-smoking, beer-drinking, pistol-firing, and messy hand jobs at the burned-down house with Raven, but when he finally opens his mouth, he barely manages a whisper.

"My girlfriend," he says, "fucked me over."

"Ouch," Hedrick replies, grimacing.

Kyle snorts. "Like you could even know."

"Hey," Hedrick says. He removes his silver wristwatch, slides it into his shirt pocket. "I've been around. And if you feel like talking, I'm game."

"Fuck no," Kyle replies. He regrets the vulgarity immediately. The blasphemous tough-guy act, he knows, is stupid. Embarrassing, even. But it's all he has left. Anything less would seem like surrender.

Hedrick pushes out his bottom lip and nods. He raises himself up, then hops out of the hole. There's dirt on the seat of his pants, but he doesn't even try to wipe it off. "Well," he says, "better get back to work. Before you know it it'll be time for supper." Then he extends his arm, and though Kyle wants to take hold of Hedrick's square, outstretched hand, squeeze it hard as Hedrick pulls him out, he rises on his own, forgetting the pages of the letter that have stuck to his damp shirt, pages that, once he's upright, a gust of wind knocks loose.

The pages—all five of them—go flying. Kyle reaches out to grab one, but he's too slow. Hedrick's short and stumpy but he is not slow, he's actually surprisingly quick for a little man, and he darts after them, unaware, Kyle thinks, that he's chasing pages that probably want to be lost.

"Let 'em go!" Kyle yells, smearing dirt on his jeans and climbing out of the hole, but Hedrick raises a hand, as if to say, "I got it," even as one of the pages, as though yanked by an invisible thread, heads skyward. "Fuck it!" Kyle screams, but Hedrick's undeterred, Hedrick's committed to helping no matter how many profanities Kyle throws his way, Hedrick's a surprisingly agile old fart who cuts back and forth like he does when he refs Hawaiian Football, snagging the pages one by one, stuffing them under his arm, until only one remains, and that one's caught in the netting of a distant soccer goal, twitching in the wind. Kyle and Hedrick are about the same distance away from the goal, and when Hedrick shoots Kyle a look like *I'll race you*, Kyle can't help but take off. He's never been much of a runner, and really he should probably conserve his energy—after all, he's not done with his digging—but he can't help himself, he runs for all he's worth, riding his boot-heavy legs across the field, kicking up turf, determined, for no good reason, to be the first to reach the last page, forgetting, at least for the time it takes to cross the field, that there's a hole with his name on it that has to be filled.

MAN-O'-WAR

I don't know why I keep leaving these messages, but for a second, when your voice comes on and you say, Hey ya'll, this is Tavey Preston, leave me your number and I'll get back to you, I trick myself into thinking, Hey, maybe she will, so I wait for the beep and when it comes I start talking, expecting, at some point, to hear another beep, then the dial tone, but I don't, never have. It's almost encouraging. Like huh, the voicemail isn't cutting me off, maybe I should keep talking. So I do, so I am, even if I've been feeling proud for not having called in a while. Today, though, I don't even know how to start talking about today, so I'll just start from the beginning. Today begins with a woman from Happy Top, a woman I've never seen and whose name I wouldn't remember. She comes into the office, lies back in the chair, opens her mouth, and releases the kind of stink you'd expect from a lower intestine. I look inside, wonder what the hell's she been eating? Firecrackers? Because every tooth in her head's black or decayed or worn down to a nub. Thing is she's only concerned about one tooth, a lower back molar, number seventeen. She points to it, says *this* is the one she wants out. Which blows me away. I'm thinking, get it over with, extract 'em all, start over. But no. She's wants seventeen out and that's it. I don't have time to argue, so I go ahead with the injection, tell her to sit tight. In the next room sits Peg Haversham, a three-hundred-pound woman whose face couldn't be flatter if she pressed it against a pane of glass. First thing she says is, You ain't gonna stick me today, are you? And I say, Well, if you behave we won't have to. Because that's the kind of person Peg is: she needs you to give her a hard time. Well, she says, thinking

—53—

about the stick, I can promise a lot but I don't know if I can promise you that. She turns to Sherrill, my assistant, says, You know that's my boyfriend. And Sherill says, Is that right? Yes ma'am, Peg replies, but if he don't start treatin' me right, I may have to leave 'im. Which is funny and also sad because Peg's probably never been kissed, never even held anybody's hand, much less *left* anyone. Open, I say. Peg opens, reveals one of the biggest tongues I've ever seen. This tongue, it's powerful. A stinky, plaque-caked slug ramming itself against whatever it runs up against: my fingers, the mirror, the explorer. I fight and dodge the tongue, adjust her crown, promise to treat her better, then return to room one, check the bombed out woman's mouth, poke around, ask can she feel anything. She can. I'm thinking *come on, I'm behind, don't need this gimme-extra-Novocaine bullshit*. I give up another injection, a little less carefully this time, wait a minute, poke. Finally, tooth's numb, I wrench it back and forth, pop it out, pack the socket, send her on her way. Doesn't hit me until over an hour later: I extracted the wrong tooth. Second to last molar, yes, but on *the wrong fucking side*. Got *thirty-two*, not seventeen. Why didn't she say something? Was she scared? Stupid? Who knows. I figure she doesn't know why I did what I did, but I'm the dentist, I did something, she'll live with whatever it was. This is the best explanation I can muster while hovering over the mouth of a girl who's waiting for me to pull a loose tooth. Normally, a loose tooth wouldn't qualify as urgent, but the girl's mother's fighting the urge to puke at the sight of a bone wobbling in her daughter's head, doesn't laugh when I trot out the old *you know, you don't have to brush all your teeth, just the ones you want to keep*. I yank out the loose tooth, pack the hole with gauze, prescribe an ice-cream sundae and two hours of cartoons, then head toward the front desk, where I plan to instruct Daphne to track down the lady with the bombed-out mouth, get her to come back, so I can take out the right tooth. I end up not reaching the desk because Daphne's in the hallway, cradling a torso-sized cardboard box in her arms. Hey, Doc, she says, you been keeping something from us? I frown, as if the box presents an actual mystery. Meanwhile, my head's tingling with electricity, thinking: *the pictures...* because I know the pictures—our pictures, the ones from the wedding—are inside that box. Daphne points to the address label. It says *Dr. & Mrs. Ted Barber*. Who, she wants to know, is Mrs. Ted Barber? Huh, I say, that's weird, and then, No, okay, *Mrs. Barber*, that's my mom. See, I explain, Mom and Dad are coming for a visit, and Mom, she's nuts about ordering stuff. It's a real problem. She orders so much and she's so worried about what she orders that when she goes on vacation or even visits people she has whatever it is she's ordered shipped to wherever she knows she's gonna be. Daphne buys this, or seems to, because she shrugs and hands me the package, which looks like it's taken a real beating, like it's been flown around the world a couple thousand times—you know how cardboard boxes get when they're worn down and crumbly around the edges, when they're barely holding themselves together? I thought after all this time the box had been lost in the mail, even hoped it *was* lost, not because I didn't want to see the pictures but because I knew looking at them would kill me. And today, they finally arrive in a bashed-up box, which I can't open, because I don't want to fall apart there in the office and because I haven't told anybody about you. About *us*. The only person who knew about us before I moved to town was Don Guiness; you remember, the realtor? The fat man with big pores and a nose that whistled when he breathed? That guy.

The one I asked to take your name off the mortgage, the one who said yeah, his wife'd left him, too, and I left it at that. Not that I didn't want to talk about you—I just didn't know how. Now, it's easier not to. What am I supposed to say when someone asks? Yeah, you know, I *was* married before—but not for long, because after the wedding, my wife and I, we went to Mexico, where I got sick, and my wife tried to take care of me, but I was an idiot, because I was convinced my sickness was a sign, we were doomed, none of this would work out, which, hey, whattaya know, on the third day, we got into an argument and she went swimming in the ocean to cool off, and she swam out really far, got stung by a Portuguese man-o'-war, had a bad reaction to the poison, went into anaphylactic shock, and, as she tried to swim back, drowned. It'd be fine if people were simply wowed by this story, if they said something like, That's the most fucked up thing I ever heard. But people aren't simply wowed. More often they're *sorry*. They want details, the gorier the better, because gory details, that shit fuels their sympathy. Long story short? Don't bring it up. But today, I came close. Today, when Daphne asked who's Mrs. Barber, my muscles in my mouth contracted, ready to answer. Thankfully, I kept my mouth shut. Because no matter how much you like your employees, you need to maintain distance, especially if they aren't going to be employees much longer, which Daphne is not. Which sucks because I'd love to keep her. So she's not always great with patients, doesn't always help the seniors to their cars, can't seem to remember that you shouldn't eat cheese balls while totaling up someone's bill or use the computer for messaging your friends who haven't been kicked out of high school. She's still funny, does a great impersonation of that guy from *Sling Blade*, never complains about work, might not remember to empty the trash or respond to the Autoclave beep, but also doesn't seem like she'd lift bills from the cash drawer. It'd be easier if she didn't have a fourteen-month-old baby or a grandmother who's been laid off by the Lee Plant or if I could say that if that were me, in her situation, I wouldn't feel entitled to a few twenties now and again, especially if I didn't have a car, which Daphne doesn't. Today, though? Her not having a car buys her some time. The plan was I'd sit her down after work, explain I'd gone through the books, that we'd been short every day since June, and I had no choice but to let her go. Then, around two o'clock, it starts drizzling. By five, it's pouring. We haven't had a storm in weeks, so you'd think this'd be good, except I don't have the heart to fire Daphne, then send her home on foot in a downpour. So we wait out the storm in the lab. I pretend to torch a few clay models I've already torched and Daphne watches a special on Animal Planet about a baby hippopotamus who falls in love with a hundred-year-old tortoise. She keeps saying you don't need to stay, I can close up, and I keep saying, no, it's okay, I've got work to do, which I don't, but I'm not crazy, no way am I leaving her alone in this office. After an hour, though, I can't take it. Come on, I say, I'm driving you home. I set the alarm, we race to the door, dash across the parking lot. I unlock the Maxima, we dive in, soaked, our breath steaming the windows. Daphne's looking around, like this is her first time in an automobile. She runs her hands over the dash, asks how many miles it has, how many it gets to the gallon, how fast I've taken it, what kind of music do I listen to, etc. I punch power on the CD player. Inside it's one of your mixes, the one that goes: *Women of the world, take over, because if you don't the world will come to an end*. Daphne's bobbing her head to the music, telling me which way to turn, glances into the back seat, wonders what's in the bag and can she take a look? Sure, I say, not wanting to seem like a guy who has a bag he wouldn't want anyone else rummaging through. She hauls the bag into the front, opens it, starts digging. My stomach drops; it's the bag with your clothes. The old T-shirts that say *Terrapins*, the jeans, the concert tees, the button-ups, all your favorites are there. Daphne holds up a sports bra, says, Doc? And me, face totally deadpan, I say right, those are my sister's, accidentally picked them up during the move, was gonna mail them home, but when I called to get her address she said, Toss 'em, they were headed to Goodwill anyway. Really, Daphne says, she was gonna throw all this stuff out? Yeah, I say, and then, You want them? Sure, Daphne says. I say, Take the whole thing. Daphne slides her hand onto mine, squeezes it. Thanks, she says. Forget it, I say. Seriously, she says, you're so sweet. She wants to thank me for everything, for giving her a chance, for believing in her, for knowing that just because she didn't have any work experience didn't mean she couldn't do a good job. As her thumb strokes my thumb, my first thought isn't *wow, this girl who's been stealing from me is supremely manipulative*, it's that this girl, this admittedly quite attractive and extremely young girl with freezing, but very soft, hands, *Is she coming onto me*? And if she is, could this actually *work*? Ha! The answer is no. Daphne's a kid, barely eighteen. She eats baloney sandwiches and watches *The Batchelor* and used to accompany her boyfriends on friggin' *coon* hunts. Last year, she drove her friend's Camaro into the side of a house. Her whole life, she's never earned higher than a C, never been further west than Chattanooga, and that was in fifth grade, when her homeroom visited the aquarium. Daphne's a kid, a baby with a baby of her own. But that doesn't keep me from thinking: *So what if we weren't meant to be?* Maybe we were meant to wreck each other, learn something profound about how fucked-up people are. Maybe we'd have amazing sex or discover we could lay in the dark and reveal the worst things we'd ever done or thought. Maybe I'd learn how to be a father to Caleb Christopher, who's always seemed, whenever Daphne's mawmaw's brought him around, like an angel, if not very bright, a kind of slobbery cherub made for bouncing on someone's knee. As I'm picturing this chubby, salivating child, Daphne removes her hand, points to the left, says, Turn here, follow this road up to the first trailer on your right, watch out for the potholes. Which I do. Minutes later, I'm parking in front of a corrugated single-wide bearing out-of-season Christmas lights. I ask Daphne if she needs help with the bag and she does, so I tote it. The front window's fogged up; leaves of dying houseplants lick the inside of the panes. I'm flooded with that empty, nauseous feeling you get when you drink too much caffeine and don't eat. We step inside. The bag's so heavy it starts to rip; I plop it on the carpet. Caleb Christopher's in his chair, sucking on a bottle of dark liquid, Coke maybe, hopefully Diet, so his teeth don't turn into eraser nubs before he turns fourteen. Caleb Christopher spots Daphne, starts to wail. Daphne's mawmaw, a liver-spotted woman with wobbly hands and transparent green tubing snaking around the side of her recliner, says, He's good as gold all day, saves his crying for when his momma gets home, which makes total sense to me, since if I was a baby drinking Coke in a house that felt like a thousand degrees with an old woman smoking cigarettes, I'd probably cry, too, once my mama finally appeared. Hey mawmaw, Daphne says, look at these clothes Doc give me. She dumps everything onto the singed brown carpet. Daphne bounces the baby on her knee, as if she intends to shake every last tear from Caleb Christopher's vibrating head. With her one free hand, she unfolds your clothes: the *Cancer 5K Run* shirt, the velvet high school letter jacket, the sweaters and jeans and turtlenecks. I stand there as she spreads them on the floor, hands on my hips, wanting to escape, not knowing when to say I should get going. Mawmaw lights a cigarette, exhales enough smoke to fill the room. Daphne says she wants to try some of these on, wait right here, disappears down the hall. I ask Mawmaw how she's doing. Mawmaw says, Purty good, been better, been worse, don't have much to complain about today and you? I say I'm fine and we watch Vanna White turn the last vowel of the phrase Expectant Fathers. A few minutes later, Daphne's back, says the skirt's a little big but I like it. She's wearing that white sweater and black skirt of yours, both wrinkled, and I say, Wow that looks great because it does. I take a deep breath, swear I can smell Chanel mixing with the smell of Mawmaw's smoke and whatever fatty slab of meat's crackling in the oven, wonder if the way Daphne's biting her lip is some kind of invitation, realize if I don't get out of there fast I'll regret it. The only thing I've eaten all day is a blueberry Pop-Tart, but I say no thank you to biscuits and green beans and ham and mashed potatoes; I gotta get home. Back in the Maxima, I try to draw up a plan in my mind for supper, think, *maybe McDonald's*, since that's the only restaurant in town with a drive-through. Only, I can't eat at McDonald's without acknowledging that you would not, even under the most dire of circumstances, eat there, and I'm not in the mood to feel any guiltier than I already do, especially since later I've got to open that package, which I've almost forgotten about. So I'm heading down Main Street, past the old Piggly Wiggly, where the faded sign has big holes from kids launching rocks into the pig's face, and I spot that health food store on the left, you know, the one we tried to go into before, when we looked at houses last winter? We tried to see in but didn't realize until we got close that it was closed and the windows had been blinded with trash bags? *Today*, I think, *today's the day to pay Better Way Health Food Store a visit.* Turns out, the place isn't much of a store. The selection's sparse, the shelves are dusty, the walls decorated with posters of Mary and bleeding Jesuses. A dot matrix sign above the cash register says, *If you smoke in here I'll hang you by your toenails and pummel you with an organic carrot.* The owner's this old wiry guy with oversize glasses and a bald head. He looks like a turtle who's lost its shell, and when I walk in he's dubbing a cassette tape on a special tape-dubbing machine, and the sound is the sound of a man talking on fast-forward about a mineral supplement that will stop the body from decomposing. Turtle Man doesn't notice me at first, and when he does he yells, Ever tried my Tiger Milk? Because if I'm interested he's got a fresh batch in the cooler. By cooler, he means the industrial-sized refrigerator at the back. Inside there's a clear jug with a strip of masking tape on it. Tiger Milk, it says. I help myself to one of the little Dixie cups, hold it under the jug spout, press the push button. A thick stream plops into the cup. I shoot it. It's nasty, but bearably so. Nutty, milky, with traces of sediment. Turtle Man asks what do I think. I smack my lips. Not bad, I say. It's a mocktail, he says. What? *Mock tail*, he says again, a fake cocktail. It's got brewer's yeast in it, he says. Mm, I say. I'm wondering why wherever I go is a place I want to leave, but I feel sorry for this guy, alone in here with expired supplies, making tapes about longevity. I ask how business is going. He says he prays every day to the Lord to send him customers. I want to tell him it looks like the Lord might not give a damn, but a voice in my head rebukes me, says I might be this guy's answer to prayer, so I buy a jar of Tiger Milk and a loaf of lentil bread, thinking, *lentils are good, I could use the protein*, say good-bye to Turtle Man, never explain who I am, enjoying the anonymity. Back at the cabin, it becomes apparent that lentil bread needs to be washed down, but the only liquid I've got besides water and expired milk and a tiny bit of OJ which is mostly backwash is a bottle of Old Grandad, so I pour myself half a mug, then fill it, thinking, fuck it, *let's kill two birds with one stone*, one, swallow the lentil bread and two, acquire some courage for package opening. Half a mug later, I'm sliding a key through the box tape when the phone rings. Normally, I wouldn't bother, what with the readout flashing *MOM & DAD*, but the timing's so perfect I trick myself into thinking it might be important. I pick up the phone. Hey, Bear, Mom says, like she always does. Hey, I say. So, she says, what would you think about us coming down next weekend? What she means to say is, Can we come see you, take care of you, buy you stuff, shower you with gifts, help you fix up the cabin, anything that'll let us feel more like parents? Which pisses me off. I know she wants to see me, always does, never hasn't wanted to. But more than that, it's her need to be needed, to accomplish some motherly task, to feel useful. She can't accept that there's nothing for her to do, can't acknowledge that acknowledging there's no way to comfort me might offer the comfort she desires to give. I don't have the balls to tell them, Don't come down, won't admit I can't stand the sight of them, so I say, Now's not such a good time. Then, to distract Mom from further lines of questioning, all of which will no doubt lead to tears, I ask if she's gotten the pictures, knowing she hasn't because the pictures, or what I'm pretty sure are the pictures, are sitting on the table in the kitchen, inside a box I'm poking with a dirty fork in order to open, if possible, a little peephole. No, she says, hasn't gotten anything, wonders if she should call the photographer, because, Ted, you paid good money for those. Ah, I say, I paid good money for a lot of things. My honeymoon, for example. Ted, she says. For instance, I say, I also recently paid good money for a man-o'-war. Silence. You know, I continue, a Portuguese man-o'-war, the invertebrate, I bought one. No you didn't, she says, and I say, Okay, I didn't, meaning, yes I did, though actually I haven't, since purchasing a man-o'-war hasn't occurred to me until now. But mom buys it, or seems to, because afterwards, there's silence. Or almost silence. Almost-silence punctuated with clickety-clicks, meaning Dad's on the phone, playing Solitaire, his favorite pastime when eavesdropping, though this time he's managed to find a topic to weigh in on. He wants to know where I found a man-o'-war, if it's legal to own one, who I ordered it from, how it was shipped, etc., so I keep the whole scenario going, explaining that there's a shop downtown that can order any animal or animal product in the world, because the guy who owns the shop runs this hush-hush kind of business where, under the right auspices and slipping through the right loopholes, he can acquire anything from a platypus to actual tiger's milk. So, I say, I ordered a Man o' War, and a couple of days ago it arrived, via UPS, in a cooler. Dad wants to know how I can find an aquarium big enough and I say, It's a baby one, and Mom wonders what I feed it and I say, Goldfish, and she says, That's sad, and I say, Of course it's sad, it's supposed to be sad, that's the whole point, that's why I got the fucking thing in the first place. Which shuts her up. And because I can't resist hurting her, no matter how much I love her, because she needs to be hurt, maybe even longs to be, I say the man-o'-war's actually four different creatures in one. Its sail, I explain, or bladder, is a balloon filled with gas, which allows it to float, and also to move, since it has to rely on the wind as a propellant. But, I continue, there are other parts, too, like the tentacles, which are filled with poison. When a fish swims by, the stingers paralyze it, and the prey's digested by polyps. Actually, I say, I've been thinking of stinging myself, of putting my hand in to see how it feels. Don't be ridiculous, Mom says. You're being ridiculous and you're saying things that don't make sense, so just tell us, is next weekend really not good. No, I say, it is not. Not next weekend and probably not the next or the next after that. Fine, Mom says, we won't come, you'll never see us again, are you happy now? She hangs up. Then it's me and Dad, and me listening to Dad, who's not saying anything but hasn't stopped his Solitaire game, so what I get is an intermittent series of clicks. After a while, I wonder if he's forgotten to hang up the phone, but then he says, You know, drowning's supposed to be a great way to go. The phrase stuns me a little, not unlike a poison zap to the head. *A great way to go*, I think. Go meaning die. Great meaning, if you're gonna die, might as well drown. Clearly, he's not offering this as comfort. It's more like: hey, I heard this fact, isn't it interesting? And it is. Some days, when I'm staring into somebody's mouth, face to face with a bloody hole, I imagine what it might've been like to swim into a man-o'-war, the crush of water, then the shock of the tentacles, the resultant burning and cramping, the need to reach the shore, and eventually the realization that this was it, this was the end unfolding, though maybe after the poison made it all the way to your heart, your brain slowed down your perception of time, and you had a kind of vision, and in this vision you were able to experience a lifetime's worth of events, your brain flash-forwarding through a series of could've-beens. And maybe, even though it's been three months since you died, if you were to compare my perception of time and your perception of time, whatever dream opened up in the ark of your head is just beginning. The man-o'-war, bobbing around thoughtlessly. You, approaching it unknowingly. You, having no idea what you hit when those tentacles scorched you, and the man-o'-war having no idea what it hit, either, since the man-o'-war, although resembling a wrinkleless brain attached to a string of nerve cords, never knows what it's getting when something gets tangled in its tentacles. And me, three months after the fact, standing here in the kitchen that should've been ours, holding a package that I can't open, talking to you, pretending you can hear what I'm saying. It doesn't make me feel any better, doesn't make me feel any worse. The sound of my voice, actually, is better, sometimes, than the sound of the crickets at night, or the sound of the wind, or of the house creaking, settling in, making whatever adjustments houses make. The fact is, me talking about this only means that I'm avoiding what I called to say in the first place, which is that I'm not going to open the package, I'm going to put it in the cellar, where I've stacked the rest of our wedding presents, and then I'm going to come back up and take a handful of Valium and lay in our bed and wait for the glow. You're invited, of course. You always are. I know I used to say the dead are dead and all that, but lately, it seems, I'm changing my tune. The texts, so to speak, are open to interpretation. It's not like I'm getting my hopes up. I know better than that, hopes up being part of what always gets me down. The one thing I won't let go of, the thing I can't give up, not yet at least, is these calls. I'd like to be able to say I know for a fact you'll never hear any of this. It used to be I had enough arrogance to believe that. Now, though, I don't know. As the time unfurls, it seems less and less possible that I can't reach you, that the dark I'm in can't be lit by your body. That's why I keep talking. Why I keep calling. I think maybe one day you'll answer. And really, what do I have but time. What do I have left to do but wait.

THE GOSPEL OF MARK SCHNEIDER

On Laura's first day at the Purdue entomology lab, while she was counting white larvae floating in glass vials, Mark asked her if she was gay, and she said yes. Based on her first ten minutes of observing him, she'd thought he was a cocky asshole. She liked him immediately.

"Does the fact that I'm gay bother you?" She smiled.

"Ain't none of my business," he said, grinning and shaking his head. "You know?"

Actually, she didn't know, because she was making the whole thing up. And because it made him smile, she let him believe it was true.

Her boyfriend, Jared, had thought she was gay at first. Yes, she had short hair. Yes, she dressed kind of like a boy. But no, she wasn't gay. She'd had an encounter with a girlfriend once, but only because she had been drunk in a bathroom and the girlfriend grabbed her face and kissed her. The waifish Jared, with piercings and bleached blonde hair, was a little androgynous himself. But she thought it worked for someone who was a lead singer for Narcoleptic and a floor manager at Best Buy.

Mark Schneider was tall, tan, and lean. He wore high tops, and baggy jeans with tight gray T-shirts that said ARMY. He spoke in a soft low voice, unless you asked him to repeat himself, and then he spoke very loud, as if he were angry, though he was only playing. When people he knew came into the lab, he stood up and shook their hands, or hunched over like a boxer, bit his upper lip, and punched them softly in the shoulder. He lived on the outskirts of Lafayette, in a prefab house with his sister and her husband and their little boy.

"Little kid loves me," Mark said, frowning. "Calls me Hee-Hee. I drive him around sometimes. He says, 'Vroom, Hee-hee, vroom!'"

Laura's second day on the job, as they counted soybeans, Mark made a confession: he was repenting. Laura asked what he'd done. He said what he'd done didn't matter. It had just come to him one day—a voice saying it was time to make things right.

"How do you know what's right?" she wanted to know.

"Bible," he said.

She shrugged. She wrote sixty-nine on the envelope and poured the beans inside. Mark wanted a change; she could understand that. She had once craved spiritual transformation—and maybe she still did. But she'd given up on church. All the changes she sought now were physical: she wanted to be thinner, she wanted long hair, she wanted to be pleasured. That, and she wanted Molly gone.

Molly was a fat girl with dyed black hair and purple makeup who'd moved in with Laura and Jared because Molly's roommate had been shipped to detox and now Molly couldn't afford her Wabash Landing apartment. The day she arrived, Molly brought a suitcase of black skirts, jewelry, and Marilyn Manson T-shirts, three boxes of videotapes, and a laundry basket full of houseplants. She plopped down on the couch and watched a video a friend of hers had made—an online sex guru named Dominique—depicting how to explore S and M safely and responsibly.

"Does she have to watch those when we're at home?" Laura asked.

Jared, still in his blue Best Buy polo, eating a banana, raised his eyebrows and said, "Laura, she's our guest. Let's please try to make her feel at home."

During her interview, Barry, the man who would become Laura's boss, had explained that being a Field Research Technician wouldn't be easy. "Some days," he'd said, smiling and staring at the ceiling as if a picture were unreeling there, "the corn will be over your head. The sun will beat down on you. You'll be swattin' at mosquitoes. Sweat'll be drippin' into your eyes."

Barry Fischer was a scientist. He was detailed, precise, and methodical; his missions required accuracy and efficiency. He wanted his employees to have all the information they could, which sometimes meant a thirty-minute lecture about how to properly clean the floor mats of university trucks. A skinny little man with big glasses and a white beard and a baseball cap and a Members Only jacket, he resembled a shell-less turtle, though he was not slow.

"Other days," he'd continued, "you'll be wading through a soybean field. That soybean field will be waist high. It's like walking through Jell-O. You ever walked through a waist high field of Jell-O?"

"No."

"Does this sound like your kind of work?" he asked. He grinned. His big teeth were yellow. Like corn.

"Absolutely," she said, though she'd never worked a day in her life. Nothing, at least, that required dirt or sweat.

Her third day at the lab, the entire team of Purdue University Field Crops Entomology Research Technicians— Mike, Raven, Brent, Trent, Molly, and Laura—scissored tiny circles in screens for bug traps. Rick, one of the head entomologists, was going to Belize to gather maggots, and he wanted to make sure they could breathe.

"You're doing it wrong," Mark said, wrinkling his nose, grinning, and nodding towards her scissors.

"What are you gonna do? Tell on me?"

"Don't never tell on anyone, man," Mark said, squinching his mouth shut.

"Why not?" Brent asked. Brent was a pudgy master's student in entomology who always wore a Cubs hat and T-shirts proclaiming the triumphs of beer. Divorced with two kids, he usually led the monologues that were to be their conversations: My ex got ahold of my credit cards. My ex gained forty pounds. My ex feeds my kids Cheese Whiz and R.C. Cola. My ex is a slut. My ex this. My ex that.

"Man, never, ever, ever rat on anyone," Mark said. "I don't care what you done." He told them about what his unit at boot camp did once when one of the geeks ratted on his friends for smoking: they had all slid padlocks into their pillowcases and each had taken a turn swinging them against the guy's head. When they were finished, the guy's face caved in. The worst part? He survived.

Laura watched Mark scissor out a perfect hole in the screen. His hands were chapped and rough.

"What?" he asked.

"You have nice hands," she said.

"Thank you," he said, batting his eyelashes.

On Laura's fourth day of work, she and Brent went to the areawide research site to plant beetle traps. They walked mile long fields, carrying shovels and long wires with plastic flags at the end. They tripped over clumps of dirt. They dug holes, inserted the stainless steel traps. Inside the traps they set bottles of antifreeze. The plan was that the beetles would tumble into the traps and be preserved by the green fluid. When the trap was set, they stabbed a wire flag into the ground, so when the corn got high, they could find the traps, and so farmers wouldn't run over them.

"What do you think of Mark?" Brent asked.

"He's pretty cool," she said.

"You know he got kicked out of the military."

"Why?"

"Nobody knows except Barry."

"What do you think he did?"

"I think he probably messed somebody up pretty bad."

Laura blinked. She remembered the story Mark had told the day before: once, Mark and his friend Matt had been going into the woods to play paintball, and they'd come upon a band of Satanists. The Satanists were in black robes around a fire and they were chanting —no kidding—"Hail Satan." Mark and Matt fired the paintball guns at them. The Satanists dispersed, swatting at their bodies, crying out for mercy. They gave them none.

Laura had believed the story, but when she thought about it now, she wondered. Mark had unbelievable stories, but he didn't seem like a liar.

Her shovel blade slid into dry, crumbly earth. Mark and another faceless man tumbled through her head. She imagined wrestling him, imagined being taken down. She worked the dirt harder.

Laura told Jared about Mark on a Friday night. They were sitting in the cushy, squeaky chairs of the Eastside movie theater, watching the lame, pre-previews trivia flash across the screen. "Wow," Jared said. "This Mark guy sounds really cool. Maybe we could get together and he could crush our skulls with a padlock in a pillowcase." Laura said he was more complicated than that: he had a little nephew; he played basketball; he was repenting. Jared finished off the popcorn and laughed and the lights dimmed and an ad for a movie with Penelope Cruz came on. Penelope wore a dress that fluttered and she pouted toward the Mediterranean. Then, as she often did when sitting in the dark in front of a flickering screen, Laura fell asleep.

At work, Mark always drove the entomology team to the ag sites. He drove the van, the truck, and the suburban. He drove whatever it was they rode in—Barry always tossed him the keys. When Mark drove, he cranked up the radio. It was obvious he wanted to be in control, which was fine with Laura—she had faith in him. It was different riding with Jared, whose slow and careful driving made her flinch. She rode in the front with Mark and they bobbed their heads to gritty power chords as the Indiana fields slid past. They gripped the oh-shit handles when fishtailing on the gravel. "Yeah," Mark said, his nose squinched up. "Yeah!"

On Laura's seventh day at work, it rained. "When it rains," Mark said as he drove the crew out to the entomology barn, "we work on the coffins." The coffins were large wooden boxes meant to house Brent's stainless steel beetle traps. Mark had spray-painted one orange then sprayed ENTOLOGY, graffiti-style, on the side.

Mark laughed when Laura picked up a drill. "What?" she asked.

"Go ahead," he said. Laura drilled two perfect holes. Mark pushed out his bottom lip and nodded. "You have a girlfriend?" he asked. Laura smiled and told him that was none of his business. He shrugged.

"Her name's Molly," she said.

"What's she look like?"

"Well, she's about three times as big as me. She's very manly. She plays on the rugby team. She listens to Marilyn Manson. Dresses in all black." She realized she should've told him that she was blond and tall with long legs, big tits.

"Have you told your parents?"

"No," she said.

"Are you gonna?"

"I'm not crazy," Laura replied, pushing the hot drill bit into the wood.

The day after the Fourth of July, Mark, who was usually early, wasn't in the lab when Laura arrived, so Barry gave Laura the keys to the Suburban and she drove out to the Purdue Ag Center, where the entomology team cut swaths in the corn plantation at the Monsanto plot. She told herself it was fun and tried to imagine what Mark would do. "Take your hoe blade and slice off the stalks," she whispered to herself, imitating his low voice. "Swing the hoe round and round like a gladiator."

In the distance, heads bobbed in and out of the green.

Mark showed up at noon, just before they took lunch.

"Laura," he said faintly.

"Why are you whispering?" she whispered back. She swatted a mosquito.

"I got laryngitis."

"How'd you get laryngitis?"

"From yelling all night."

"Why were you yelling?"

"We partied at Navy Pier. It was fun, man." He raised his eyebrows. "Real fun."

"Oh yeah?" she asked. "How fun?"

"Five blow job fun."

Laura flinched. "Excuse me?"

Mark glanced over his shoulder, then motioned for Laura to come closer. "I got five blow jobs," he whispered.

"Five?"

"Five," he whispered, grinning, his jaw jutting out. "Gospel truth." Laura frowned, trying to imagine what this could mean. She yanked a Jimsonweed out of the ground. Bits of dirt pelted her in the face. She hadn't given five blow jobs in her entire life. The look on Mark's face suggested she hadn't granted them the importance they deserved.

"Laura," he whispered.

"Yeah?"

"I don't really have laryngitis," he said in his normal voice. She punched him in the shoulder. He laughed. She punched him again.

At home, Molly was on the couch, eating a low fat yogurt, aiming the remote at the television: a rerun of Saturday Night Live. She was wearing one of Jared's band's shirts, which was weird because the shirt was not black, it was red, and it was a known fact that Molly wore only black.

"How's it going?" Laura asked.

Molly shrugged. She spooned a glob of pink yogurt onto the silver ball on her tongue. She laughed at the television. Phil Hartman was doing Caveman Lawyer. "Christ," Molly said, shaking her head.

"How's the apartment hunting?" Laura asked.

"I think I've found a place."

"I bet that's a relief," Laura said.

"Yep."

Laura headed for the shower. There was dirt under her

nails and her arms were stinging and her back was sore. In the shower, she thought of Mark, wandering the earth for blowjobs and fights. Soap stung her eyes. She held both eyes open and let the water come in.

On her fourteenth day of work, they dug up corn roots. Mark took off his T-shirt and tied it around his head. Laura did the same, even though her sports-braed torso revealed little bulges of cottage cheesey fat. Mark's torso was lean and hairless and tanned and defined. His nipples were tiny erect points. Laura wondered how many had tongued them. His right pec had a tattoo on it—some kind of Chinese character. "What's it mean?" she asked.

"Can't tell you," Mark said, his mouth sphinctering up. The tattoo looked cool there on his pecs—smooth and mysterious, and she fought an urge to touch it with her thumb. Instead, she slapped him in the back of the head. "Sorry," she said, and he slugged her softly in the belly, which made her flinch: he would know, now, how soft she really was.

On the twenty-fourth day, they dug up little troughs around young corn plants and dropped squirming black caterpillars inside, and covered them gently with dirt. The caterpillars had been Fedexed in plastic tubs. In a few hours, thanks to Dow Chemical, they would begin dying. "Death," Laura said, mashing one into the dirt.

"Yeah," Mark said.

"What do you think about when you think about it?"

"Heaven," he said. "Hell."

"You really believe in all that?"

"Sure," he said, holding up one of the caterpillars. It wasn't moving. "You ever go to church?" She nodded.

"Don't you remember when Jesus told his disciples, 'And if I go and prepare a place for you, I will come again, and receive you unto myself; that where I am, there ye may be also'?"

"Vaguely."

Mark snickered. "You ain't afraid of hell, are you?"

"Not enough to let some church dictate everything I do."

"I don't believe everything they teach."

"Like what?"

"Some stuff's fucked-up," Mark said, looking out across the field. "The Apostolic church, man. They don't allow you to date. You have to do stuff in groups. And when you want to marry somebody, you tell a brother, and he goes to an elder, and the elder asks the girl's father."

"Why do you go, then?"

"I told you," he said, pulling a weed from the soil. "I'm repenting."

When Laura came home that evening, Jared and Molly were playing Resident Evil on Jared's computer. Molly had already beaten the game. She was kneeling on the floor, trying to get Jared through the next-to-last level. Her arm was propped on Jared's shoulder.

"What's up?" Laura asked.

"Just a sec," Jared said, wiping his forehead with the back of his hand. "I'm about to kill this last guy." Laura waited for Molly to move her arm, for Jared to finish the game. Jared's man died at the hands of the undead. Molly clicked Reset. Laura went to the kitchen, peeled open a pudding. She told herself she didn't care. And she didn't.

On her thirty-seventh day of work, as they drove out to Muncie, Mark told Laura she should never replicate the signs he was making with his hands. She laughed. He didn't. The signs were serious. So serious he couldn't tell her what they meant. "You don't want to know," he said. He'd been in a gang, up near Gary. Those guys in Lafayette, he said, with one leg of their jeans pulled up and the handkerchiefs on their heads, they didn't have a clue about gangs. "Gangs aren't about style," he said. "They're about family."

"You were in a gang?"

"I can't talk about it."

"You can tell me. I'm cool."

"It's not about being cool, Laura. It's about protecting each other."

She waited for him to laugh, to tell her it was all one big joke, but he didn't, and when he changed the subject by telling her how the woman in the red car they'd just passed had once given him cocaine and had let him ride her four-wheeler, she let talk of gangs slip away.

"If I tell you something," Mark said, "you swear you won't tell nobody?" They were washing corn roots. The day before, the crew had driven to a site at Columbus and dug up six hundred plants. It'd been hot. Horseflies had dive bombed them. Mosquitoes had gone for their ears. They'd dug hard for a long time, numbered the roots with permanent ink, bagged them, and loaded them into a truck. Now they were spraying them with hoses and high-pressure guns that shot fine streams of stinging mist. The roots looked like baby aliens with white tentacles for hair.

"I won't tell anyone."

"Not even your girlfriend."

"Not even my girlfriend." Here it comes, she thought. I killed a man. I killed somebody. Or, I'm gay, too. Her heart rippled.

"My stepfather used to beat the living shit out of me,

Laura."

He'd gotten smacked with a screwdriver, a hammer, a brick. He told her about fights at school, about being shipped for the summer to Indianapolis, where his uncle, a gym owner, taught him to box. It was like a TNT movie. He was the Champ.

She pictured him bloody and sweaty and bruised. She imagined him victorious, unattainable, flanked by gorgeous blondes.

Jared broke up with Laura one day when she came home from work. She was stuffing her jeans and socks and T-shirt, all black with dirt, into the washing machine.

"Is it Molly?" she asked, grabbing a dirty towel from the hamper and wrapping it around her body.

"Molly? Of course not. I'm just questioning some things about my life right now. I need a change."

"Maybe you could repent," Laura said. "It seems to be working for another asshole I know."

"Laura, there's no need to—"

"Maybe you could integrate yourself into a gang."

"I can see this isn't going anywhere."

"Or, maybe you could fuck off," she said, and smirked. Jared's eyes began to tear up. He bit his lip and looked the other way. "Sorry," she whispered, trying to sound like she meant it.

Laura and Jared and Molly continued to live together. Jared slept on the floor now, but many nights Laura fell asleep to the sound of him talking to Molly in the living room, and woke up to visions of Mark evaporating.

Laura knew that once school started and she quit work, she wouldn't see Mark again. She knew he wouldn't give her his number unless she asked for it. She knew he'd give her one of those good-bye hugs big robust men give each other— the kind with the hand thud against the back—and say they should go fishing or something. And, one day, she'd try to call him. A woman would answer, and when Laura asked for Mark, the woman would say, "Wrong number."

Her last day at work, Barry asked if Laura and Mark would go up to Valparaiso to count aphids. In the fields they took off their shirts again and wrapped them around their heads. They dove into a rye field and leaped back out, and the field held an impression of their bodies. In the soybean field they found no aphids. But they weren't really looking.

"Isn't it weird that they depend on us to be, like, highly accurate, but in reality we aren't?" Laura asked.

"You think too much," Mark said. He chewed a blade of grass, blew a strand from his tongue. It landed on her arm. She flicked it away. "But you know what?"

"What?"

"It's gonna suck when you quit. Who am I going to talk to?"

"Brent?"

"Please. Brent's a fuck-up. Let's go," he said, spitting the grass out of his mouth. "We have to make a stop on the way back."

"Why are you turning off here?" she asked. They had the windows down. Creed blasted through the stereo. It was hot.

"You'll see."

She imagined Mark would stop the truck and they'd tumble into a drainage ditch. You are not a lesbian, he'd say, and she'd say, Of course not, stupid.

Instead, Mark pulled up at a small, brown, ranch-style house. Three small, unidentifiable dogs came leaping out of nowhere. "This is my mom's house," he said.

Mark's mom looked like him. Lean and dark. Thin lips. Blond hair, cut like a boy's. Inside the house Mark showed Laura a stuffed frog he'd won at the fair, a Glamour Shot of his sister wearing a cowboy hat, and a saw blade that had the seasons painted on it. "Pretty neat, huh?" He led her through the house, then out into the backyard, where there was an aboveground pool.

"I don't have a suit," she said.

"Don't matter," he said. "Just go in your clothes."

The flimsy metal ladder burned their feet and palms as they climbed up to the hot aluminum poolside. They jumped in. It was cold.

Mark said they should race across the pool. They did. He won. "We should wrestle," he said. They did. He won. He wanted to know who could hold their breath longer, who could swim farthest underwater, who could make the biggest splash. He could.

"We had a big party here once," he whispered. He glanced at his mom, who'd brought out some purple bath towels and stacked them in a chair.

"You did?"

"Yeah. Everybody took their clothes off. Everybody went skinny dipping. Everybody."

"Were there girls?" she asked, her head against his smooth, muscular back.

"Of course there were girls," he said. "You would have loved it."

He grabbed her and carried her through the water. She

closed her eyes, and held on. He lifted her out of the water. He let her fall. Then he pushed her to the bottom with his feet.

When she couldn't get up, she panicked. She thought he might be drowning her, and a picture flashed in her mind: his mother—standing over the edge of the pool, a glass of lemonade in her hand—peering into the water. Laura reached for him but her arms weren't long enough. Just when she thought her lungs would burst, he stopped.

She surged up coughing. Water dribbled from her nose. It burned. "What the fuck?"

He laughed. She punched him in the tattoo—hard. He tried to grab her arm when she went for his face, but it was slippery, and her finger went into his eye. He leaped back. She gasped. Oh God, she thought, I've blinded him.

"Let me see," she said. She was surprised when he let her look. She held open the eye. Red flesh. Veins. White ball. What had it seen?

"There's a scratch," she said. His face was so close she could see into his pores. Before she could stop herself, her lips touched his.

At first, he kissed back. But then he said, "Whoa," and eased her away. He rubbed his eye and, holding it shut, walked through the water and climbed out of the pool. Laura followed, needing to breathe heavily but trying not to.

Mark's mom had placed a bowl of muskmelon and an open bag of greasy barbecue potato chips on a table in the shade of an umbrella. She was smoking a very thin, very long cigarette. Mark held out his hand; she gave him the cigarette. He took a couple of drags, blew the smoke out his nose, then handed it back. "What's wrong?" his mom asked. He was opening and squeezing shut the hurt eye.

"Nothin'," he said.

"Let me see."

"Ma, no," he said, in his fake-stern way.

"Fine," she said. "I gotta go inside before these gnats eat me alive." She smacked her leg, but she didn't get up.

Laura ate a chip. Her hands were a little shaky, so she patted one of the mutts and grasped a handful of its fur. Mark frowned at her, pressing his thumb into his eye. Laura frowned. She took a piece of melon from the bowl. When Mark's mom wasn't looking, her tongue flicked against the pink cube wildly, as though pleasuring it. Mark grinned and, with one eye still pinched shut, shook his head. Laura chomped into the melon and grinned. The cold hurt her teeth, and as the juice ran down her chin, she wondered if, later, Mark would tell someone: Man, this lesbian totally tried to hit on me, or Man, this girl who told me she was a lesbian, but wasn't, totally tried to hit on me or Man, this girl who told me she was a lesbian, but wasn't, totally tried to hit on me, then acted like she wasn't trying to. Gospel truth. "Barry's gonna be wondering where we are," Mark said.

Let him wonder, Laura thought. It was her last day. She could lie here for a while in the chair, with the dog and the chips and the melon and the mom. She wanted Mark to tell stories, wanted a cheap, cold beer to go with them. Tell me something I don't know, she thought. Something impossible. Something I won't believe.

But there would be no more stories. Stories were over. Mark was sliding his feet into his shoes, his torso into the ARMY shirt. He kissed his mother goodbye and slung the keys to the entomology team Suburban at Laura. They stung when they hit her in the chest, but she was glad to be the one driving. She was ready to go fast with the windows down. She was ready to make Mark yell, "Slow down," ready to stomp the pedal and surge forward, their terrified laughs sucked up by the wind.

SECOND HOME

When Eva Gladstone reached the house where she lived, she accelerated past the end of the driveway, past the overgrown lawn, and past the yellow trees, upon which tiny, strangulated plastic ghosts swayed in the breeze. She slowed down only for corners, stop signs, and traffic lights. Eventually, the houses of the suburbs disappeared, and there were only trees and hills, then mountains.

She turned on the radio. In a far-away country, war had been announced. Fires were consuming the West. Hurricanes were storming the tropics. People were drowning in flames and fumes and water and earth. And she was driving a 1984 Mercedes—immaculate, polished, and freshly vacuumed, as her husband Arthur had liked to keep it—into the Land of the North.

Eva had not prepared for a journey. She had no tooth-brush and no soap—no change of underwear. She had a purse with a few pens, a wallet, some faded, slightly wrinkled pictures of her estranged son and late husband, a checkbook, some credit cards, a tube of lipstick. There was a hammer slash hatchet in the trunk and underneath the groceries purchased at Trader Joe's, some jumper cables. In the glove box: a pack of crackers, some peppermints, a few maps. That was all.

It was midafternoon when Eva arrived at Lake Sunapee. It was cold. For a minute, blue clouds rained snow. The vents blasted heat. Her hands cramped, her back ached. She coasted over hills, then turned off the highway and shot down a long unmarked road, going down, down, down very fast. She had not driven a car dangerously for a long time, and it felt good.

She administered the brake, turned off onto gravel, then pavement again: a driveway. She parked the car in front of the freestanding red garage at the top of the hill, got out, unlatched the great wooden door, swung it open, got back into the car, and drove it inside.

The green door of the cabin was unlocked, as it always had been. There was wood stacked on the porch. A stick had toppled off the pile. She replaced it.

Inside, the kitchen smelled faintly of mold. The overhead light—a yellow glass bowl at whose bottom insect shells lay—had been left on. A light burning in an empty room. For how long? She turned it off.

From the living room she could see the lake, choppy with whitecaps. The cabin was as they'd left it two, ten summers ago. Board games stacked in one corner; a Philip Roth novel on the coffee table; black-and-white pictures in wooden frames on the wall. Here, in the living room, something like relief. Clarity. Tranquility.

She sat on the dusty sofa. The springs creaked. On the coffee table, into which her son had carved his name with a pocketknife years ago—ETHAN—lay a photograph book. She picked it up. Inside: Ethan in water wings. Artie slicing a crescent into the lake on a slalom ski. Eva—dark and slender—in a bathing suit and swimmer's cap, poised to dive.

Eva walked across the room and turned on a portable radio. A Bach toccata was just ending. A man with a deep voice announced the time, then predicted the weather: wind. After midnight, a 50 percent chance of snow. She turned off the radio.

The number 3 blinked on the answering machine, but she didn't press play. She picked up the receiver on the big black rotary telephone—and dialed her home number.

Arthur's voice, not yet erased, repeated the number she'd dialed. The beep was so loud and alarming that she left a message. "Uh, I'm at the cabin," she said, imagining the still life of the house: lamps, couches, hutch, end table, the reflections of these things in the glass of the blank television. The sound of her voice going through the machine. She hung up.

Upstairs, everything was clean. Someone had left a snorkel and mask on the dresser. Everything else had been put away. The beds had been stripped. Then she noticed the suitcases—a red one duct-taped shut, another fairly new black one. There was a Bible on the nightstand. The front cover said, John Montgomery, Jr.

When she unsnapped one of the latches of the suitcases, she heard a car outside. She frowned, walked out of the bedroom, across the hall. She peeked out the window.

Outside, a black Corolla. The doors opened. The driver—a man, about fifty, robust, with salt-and-pepper hair, a mustache, and a big chin. The other door opened. The passenger wore a tattered red baseball cap, and a U.S. Postal Service jacket: her son.

Eva covered her mouth with her hands.

Eva had not lived the life of the rich and weary. She and her husband, who'd had some success in the heating-and-cooling business, had enjoyed their wealth. They were happy. They gave money away. They luxuriated.

Then they had a son.

They named the son Ethan. For the first fifteen years of his life, he was an astoundingly perfect kid. Obedient. Sweet. Selfless. Ate his vegetables, stood up straight. Cried when he got A minuses. Got up in the middle of the night because he realized he'd forgotten to put his bike in the garage or had left his crayons on the dining room table. But then, not long after Ethan turned sixteen, Artie found a Playgirl under the seat of the little Ford Escort they'd bought for him to drive to school. Artie asked him if that was the kind of thing he liked; Ethan, who couldn't help being honest, said it was. "Not in my house," Artie said. He was livid. Ethan mouthed off; Artie whipped off his belt. Ethan threw him up against the utility-room wall. There was still a perforation in the Sheetrock. An outline of the man's shoulder.

Eva had not seen her son since he'd left for California two years before. He hadn't returned for his father's funeral last spring. He had not called. And now, here he was at the family cabin, with an older man, presumably John Montgomery, Jr.

Eva slipped behind a curtain, into a closet where, on rainy days, Ethan had lit a lantern and drawn pictures of cowboys and astronauts on the walls with crayons. The drawings were invisible in the dark, and she heard the scuffle of tiny claws on wood: mice. She held her breath. She listened. Voices. The rustle of thick paper bags: groceries. The front door opened and closed. The voices were gone.

John Montgomery, Jr., and Ethan were down on the dock. The lake, like the sky, was dark. Eva could see them from the living room window. John Montgomery, Jr., checked his watch and motioned towards the cabin with his thumb.

The house creaked in the wind. Outside, airborne leaves. Trees bent back and forth wildly. Ethan's cap blew off, but he caught it. The men turned toward the house.

The back door squeaked loudly when Eva opened it. She winced.

Rather than take the peastone path that curved up to the

garage, she chose a shortcut through rhododendron bushes. She slipped and fell, her knees gouging holes into the soft earth. She stood, peeled off a few wet leaves. She could hear their voices. She hid for a moment behind a white pine. Then she continued up the hill.

Inside the garage, inside the car, she inserted the key into the ignition. She pulled it out. She inserted it again. "What the hell," she said. Then she popped the trunk, got out of the car, and carried two grocery bags down the path.

She peeked through the glass in the door. Inside, John Montgomery, Jr., tilted a Coke bottle back and took a long drink. He placed his arm around Ethan, who had discarded his cap. Ethan's hair was a mess. He stirred a steaming pot on the stove.

Eva waited for them to turn around, to see her through the window, but they never did. Her breath fogged the glass. Then she turned and walked through the woods to the cabin next door.

The cabin belonged to the Danielsons. Eva knocked. There was no answer—not at this time of year. She peeled back the welcome mat for the key and let herself in.

The last time she'd come to the Danielsons' was with Artie. It had been a very hot day in the summer. They'd spent the day on the Danielsons' boat, then returned to the house for sandwiches and beer on the Danielsons' porch. Rita and Jim got into an argument. Artie laughed. Rita tossed water in his face. The next time they all saw each other, Artie—following a brain aneurysm while atop his riding mower—was dead.

It had been six months since Arthur's death. Two weeks ago, he had appeared to Eva, not in a dream, and not at night, but in the middle of the day, after lunch. She'd been carrying a bag of trash to the garbage bin when she heard him calling her name. She turned around and saw him standing at the door of the shed. He had his work clothes on. "Eva!" he called. "Have you seen my shovel?" She dropped the bag and stared at him. She went back inside and locked the door.

Since then she had started and given up on five books. She had abandoned her baking and the garden. She had refused three invitations for dinner and two lunch dates. She stayed indoors. She cleaned. She emptied Artie's Scotch. She left the TV on but did not watch it. She tried to call her son, whom she had not seen in more than a year but she got only his machine. She left no messages.

The Danielsons had split up. Eva thought Rita had the cabin, but she wasn't sure. Like the Gladstones', this cabin offered familiar comforts—dry foods, pots, silverware, life jackets, games, quilts, sleeping bags, and pillows despondently collecting dust during the off-season, waiting patiently for vacationers to make use of them. Eva walked into the living room. She sat down at the Danielsons' air organ. She pumped the pedals with her feet, and placed her hands on the keys, but played no notes.

She opened cabinets in the kitchen. Under the sink she found an unopened bottle of Scotch. She unscrewed the top. She poured herself half a mug full, took a sip, and exhaled. In the master bedroom, she opened drawers, found a scarf, a pair of sunglasses. She tied the scarf around her head, donned the sunglasses, and slipped into one of Mr. Danielson's London Fog trench coats.

From the picnic table on the Danielsons' porch, she could see the dock of her own cabin. The man who she knew must be John Montgomery, Jr., stood on the edge with a fishing pole. He cast lines into the water. In a few minutes, Ethan, wearing one of Artie's old army jackets, joined him. John Montgomery, Jr., gave him the pole, and Ethan reeled in a fish. John Montgomery, Jr., patted him on the back, unhooked the fish, and tossed it back into the lake. The wind twisted the fishing line.

Whenever Arthur had tried to teach Ethan how to fish, Ethan ended up crying. He hadn't wanted to touch the fish. When Arthur refused to worm his hooks, Ethan stabbed his finger and let the wilting worm drop into the water.

John Montgomery, Jr., stood with his hands on his hips. When he turned around and saw Eva, he waved. Eva lifted a hand into the air, turned around, and went inside.

A knock at the door. Eva replaced the sunglasses. She expected Ethan. Instead she got John Montgomery, Jr.

"Can I help you?" she asked. He tilted his head.

"We thought we were the only ones here. John," he said, smiling and extending a hand. Up close, he was even bigger. Sturdier. Despite the fact that she did not prefer mustaches, especially the ones like his, which partially eclipsed his lips and despite the tuft of hair sticking up from the back of his head, she had to admit he was handsome. Carved and clean, as though sculpted from hard soap.

"Rita." She wiped her hand on her pants before taking his. "Please. Come in."

"Just you in here?" he said, ducking his head as he walked under the doorway.

"For now," she said, smoothing the scarf on her head.

"I saw you when we were down on the dock. My friend and I are just next door. We're cooking a big dinner. You're welcome to join us."

"I'd love to," she said, glancing at a watchless wrist. "But I have plans."

"Well, if you change your mind, you know where we are."

"Yes."

He sat down on the organ bench. "Nice place," he said, tapping one of the keys.

"Thank you."

"Boy, it's great up here, isn't it?"

"Are you a friend of the Gladstones'?" Eva asked, smiling.

"Of Ethan's."

"Where are you from?"

"California."

"You picked a strange time for a vacation."

"Ethan said it's better in the fall. The solitude and all. And the leaves."

"Just taking it easy, then?"

John Montgomery, Jr., shrugged. "Yeah. Easy. Maybe do some fishing."

"How do you know Ethan?"

"We actually work together."

"At Kinko's?" Eva bit her lip.

"How'd you know?"

"Eva and I... we talk."

"Ethan's mom."

"Yes. Have you met her?"

"No," John Montgomery, Jr., said, rubbing his chin. It made a sound like sandpaper. "I—I 'd like to. I hear great things about her."

"I'm surprised."

"Why?" John Montgomery, Jr., frowned.

"Well," Eva said, and sighed, "to tell you the truth, I didn't think she and Ethan were all that close."

"I don't think they are, really. But Ethan," John Montgomery, Jr., paused. "I think he misses her."

Eva stared out the window. Whitecaps, like teeth, on the lake.

"Would you like a drink? Water? Juice? Scotch?"

"Oh no, I'm fine," he said. "Do you play?" He nodded at the organ.

"A little."

"I love the organ."

"Are you married?" she asked, glancing at his left hand.

"Divorced. And you?"

"My husband recently left me."

"I'm sorry to hear that. I guess you know about Ethan's dad."

"I did. I attended the funeral. I didn't see Ethan there."

"Yeah," he said, nodding. "I think he might… well… I don't know."

"Yes?"

"It's complicated."

"Is it?" She unbuttoned the top button of her shirt. She smiled. "It's warm in here."

"That stove puts out the heat," he observed. The stove was not lit.

"Sure you wouldn't like a drink?"

"No thank you."

"Are you lovers, then?" Eva asked.

The man laughed—a great, hearty laugh—and slapped

his hands against his substantial thighs. But he did not answer the question. "I should probably be getting back." He smiled, politely, then he was off.

Eva sipped her drink as she watched him go. He followed the trail she'd made through the brush, pushing aside the same broken limbs.

Eva went to the window when she heard the yelling.

It was Ethan. He walked down to the dock, his hands in his pockets. John Montgomery, Jr., followed him, his head tilted, his hands held out as if quietly pleading.

John Montgomery, Jr., placed his hands on Ethan's shoulders. Ethan shrugged them away. John Montgomery, Jr., ran a hand through his hair. The wind was blowing. The leaves were almost gone. John Montgomery, Jr., turned him around, and gripped his arms firmly, and shook him as he spoke. They hugged. Then they went back inside.

Eva thought it was too cold to eat on the deck, but apparently they were dead set on it. Ethan set the table. John Montgomery, Jr., delivered a steaming bowl of pasta. They held hands and bowed their heads and closed their eyes. John Montgomery, Jr.'s lips moved for what seemed like a very long time. The steam on the pasta blew wildly away. The wind lifted a napkin into the trees, and John Montgomery, Jr., followed it.

There was no wine or beer. Only water. The two men did not light up afterwards. They sat and talked. Then they cleared the table. Ethan brought sticks of wood from the porch into the cabin. The wind never stopped blowing.

After a while the lights went out, then it was dark. The Danielsons' cabin creaked in the wind, and Eva poured the last of the bottle into her mug.

She woke, in the middle of the night, to a light dusting of snow on the ground. The clouds were gone and the moon was out. The wind had stopped. Everything was bright. She could feel her heartbeat in her throat.

If she was going to do it, it had to be now, while she was not fully awake. She saw herself winding through the trees, entering the cabin, creeping quietly up the stairs, and entering the room where Ethan slept. She would touch his hair and his face. He would wake up and stare at her, rubbing his eyes. She would embrace him. He would want to know why and how. She would say she didn't know. And, in the few minutes before he fully woke up, it wouldn't matter.

"Okay," she whispered, and flung back the covers. In the closet: another, thicker coat. It smelled of mothballs. She couldn't find her shoes. She told herself she didn't need any.

Eva walked through the woods, following the path that had been trampled. The snow melted on her feet. Leaves stuck to her ankles. Twigs poked her toes.

By the time she reached the cabin, she felt as though pins were pricking her feet. The back door was locked. She tried the front. Dead-bolted. She tried the windows. Nothing. The cold was waking her up. She panicked. She knocked on the door, quietly at first. Then she began to pound. She pounded until Ethan, in boxers and a sweatshirt, carrying a Louisville Slugger, appeared behind the glass of the door.

Ethan flipped on the outside light. He opened the door. Eva's knuckles were burning. Were they red? She was afraid to look. Her breath poured like smoke from her nose.

"Mom?"

Ethan frowned, tilting his head at his mother in a man's coat in the snow with no shoes. He squinted, wobbled. Good, she thought. He was still in the daze she'd expected. Hurry, she told herself. Catch your breath. She tried. She wheezed. Her numb feet squeaked in the snow. Ethan, standing in the doorway, clutched the bat in his fist like a boy waiting for a story he wanted to believe. Eva parted her lips to speak her son's name, as though, for the first time in his life, she might have the right words to explain.

FREEBLEEDERS

A flyer at the University of North Carolina's career center asks Kevin if he likes working with animals. He thinks he might, thinks he could, for seven dollars an hour. He had pets once, pets he admittedly cared little about, pets his father took pity on and shot with a pistol in the backyard: a cat with leukemia, a dumb retriever whose head swelled up after a rattlesnake bite, a hamster with ear rot. Kevin's not an animal lover. Never has been. It's not like he's unkind; there was that time he accidentally ran over a rabbit and he stopped to see what he'd hit and the rabbit was dragging the bloody mush of its half-crushed backside across the asphalt and he backed up, backed over it, and the girl he was with—whom he was dropping off after a promising date—screamed. He never saw her again.

Seven dollars an hour. He could stand a lot for seven dollars an hour.

It's one month after graduation, and everyone's left town. Kevin's best friend, Gary—who lived at the NORML house and hosted parties where shark meat hissed on charcoal grills and dreadlocked girls read poetry by the light of tiki torches—landed a job with Fleet Bank in Boston, where he now pulls down ten grand a month. Three weeks ago Gary flew Kevin into the city. They ate calamari at a crowded bistro in the North End, got high on hundred-dollar bottles of wine, flirted with a waitress named Michelle. This girl, she was amazing—Filipina, big smile—and she patiently indulged Kevin's drunken invitations to join Gary and him for more drinks, and possibly a few toots of cocaine. Michelle wouldn't relinquish her phone number, but Kevin persevered and left the bistro waving a napkin (bearing her email address) like a triumphant flag. Back in Chapel Hill, Kevin couldn't get her face out of his head, and even though it felt ridiculous, he made good on his promise to write. She was thrilled to hear from him, regretted not going out that night, because two days later her boyfriend had dumped her for someone else.

Now Kevin's pinned his hopes on a girl who lives a thousand miles away, a girl who continues to write during her summer in Spain, where she fails Spanish tests and parties until dawn with professional European basketball players. She sends museum-gift-shop postcards—Picasso's Guernica, Matisse's The Red Studio—the backs crammed with bubbly, exuberant script. She claims she misses Kevin. A beautiful girl Kevin hardly knows misses him! He misses her, too.

Kevin's first day at the Francis Owen Blood Research Lab, he meets Robin, the woman who manages the animal-care personnel. Her face resembles her namesake: beady eyes, beak-like nose, lipless mouth, her thin face scrubbed raw, maybe sunburned. She shows him the animals: pigs and dogs. "They're hemophiliacs," she says. "We call them free-bleeders. Their blood won't clot, so they live in cages, under the close watch of university scientists." They are, Robin claims, better off here. The outside world? Too dangerous. A scratch would send them on a slow drain toward death.

Every morning, Kevin slips into scrubs, rubber gloves, snake boots, and tries to feel important: he's a necessary cog in a scientific machine. In the Dog Den, fifty dogs live in separate kennels, pacing floors smeared with shit. Once he gets past the smell, it isn't so bad. There's something satisfying about spraying the cages clean, lasering away the fur and the shit and the piss. Rainbows appear in the mist. Sunbeams fall through the cages, latticing the lemon yellow concrete. Once he's squeegeed the cages, the dogs begin their excretions, as though it doesn't feel like home without feces.

Kevin thinks he can love the dogs; he's not sure about the pigs. Pigs, he knows, are supposed to be smart, but these are ugly and slobbery and hoofed. They nibble his pants, and when they stomp his foot it kills. Hose in hand, he wanders among them, spraying the floor, melting pig turds until they're small enough to tumble through the slats in the floor. He lassos pig snouts, holds down piglets for injections, sub-tractions, inspections. He sprays bristly hog flesh, firing shots at their flinchy ears; water foams on their backs. He wran-gles. He sweats. By break time his gloved hands are sweaty and wrinkled; through the plastic, each hair on his hand looks as dark and sharp as a stinger.

During breaks Kevin bums Camels from Brad, a quiet, tall kid with an underbite who plays guitar for a punk rock band called Killer. One day Kevin tells him about Dagwood, the spaniel who always humps his leg during cage cleanings. At first Kevin thought it was gross, then sad.

"Not necessarily," Brad says.

"What do you mean?"

"Sometimes the lab needs new dogs, right?"

"So?"

"So they make new ones."

"You mean the dogs that are here…are bred to live here?"

Brad flicks his cigarette. "Apparently," he says, "these dogs have fucked-up bloodlines running back to the seventies."

"God."

"Yeah," he replies. "It's crazy. Sometimes they breed too

many. It gets overcrowded. Then somebody gets snuffed."

Back in the Dog Den, the dogs bark and leap and pace. Their tongues drip sticky strings of saliva, their tails whap the floor. Kevin wants to be angry with Robin for not explaining, but he can't help feeling like he's duped himself: he assumed the dogs had been donated, that this was the place you brought your pooch if it wouldn't stop bleeding. Now, that idea seems impossibly naïve, or maybe just stupid. Maybe he's refused to admit what he's known all along: he's working in a broken-animal factory.

Michelle continues to write: postcards and translucent air mail stationery and a manila envelope stuffed with pictures of her partying with friends, hoisting ectoplasmic margaritas into the air. She is, Kevin realizes for the umpteenth time, extraordinarily hot; acknowledging this is ecstatically bewildering. Why is this extraordinarily hot girl writing to him? Why can't she stop thinking about him, and why would she want to come visit him when she gets back from Spain? Kevin doesn't care. He has a shoe box stuffed with correspondence from an extraordinarily hot, very sweet, totally insane girl. Everything he knows about Michelle is on paper: she likes Picasso and Matisse, wine and tequila, hip-hop and basketball, chocolate and lingerie. He wonders what she'd think if he told her about his job. All he's said is that he works at a university lab. Which is not the whole truth. He's not a lab man. He's a cage cleaner.

One day Keisha asks Kevin to help her clean dog ears. The dogs love it. Kevin holds them down while Keisha digs the Q-tip into their ear folds, scooping out great wads of golden wax. They tilt their heads, close their eyes. Keisha asks who

Kevin's favorite dog is. Kevin's never thought about this, and it takes him a minute. He guesses it's Tomata, the russet hound who always rubs her head against his leg. Keisha laughs. "She likes you, right?" Kevin shrugs. "She's got an eye infection," Keisha says. "She's using you for a scratching post."

Later that day, Ivy—a freckly scientist with prematurely graying black hair—asks Kevin and Brad to meet her at the Pig Palace. "And bring a couple of garbage cans."

When Kevin walks in, the pigs go crazy, but he's not bringing them food. Ivy stands over a cage of piglets as if admiring them. Then, with the resolute detachment true science demands, she jabs syringes full of poison into their hides. They squeal, kick, twitch, stop moving. Afterwards Kevin and Brad stuff as many cold piglets as will fit into the trash cans, pressing lids down over their moist, rubbery snouts. They roll the cans back to the lab, and deposit them inside a walk-in freezer, where they await transport.

"They go to some factory in Waxhaw," Brad explains. "They get ground up into dog food. Then they get shipped back here, for the dogs." He exhales a lungful of smoke and grins, flashing his bottom teeth. "Circle of life, right?"

"Circle of life," Kevin repeats. It's break time. He needs a Camel and a light.

Before he knows it, summer's almost over. Michelle returns from Spain, buys a ticket from Boston to Raleigh, and then there she is, emerging from gate B12 in a black dress and gold earrings. Her skin is milky chocolate; her dark eyes gleam. Her lips are just as Kevin remembered them: cherry red. A beautiful woman appears out of nowhere and he puts his arm around her, offers to carry her bag—an extravagant Hermes satchel—and she lets him. Kevin, in his holey jeans and yellow T-shirt (with a sparkly rainbow iron-on), has never felt so underdressed.

At Ramsgate Apartments, there are neither rams nor gates. There are, however, lots of awkward moments, like when Michelle visits Kevin's room for the first time and pretends to study the stuff on his walls, and he worries about what his Smashing Pumpkins posters will say about him: too maladjusted, too white, too something.

"Cool!" she exclaims. One of her postcards hangs above his desk: a toreador spearing a bull. She pulls it down and laughs. "I was so drunk when I wrote this."

Kevin wants to kiss her.

Michelle wants to make a phone call.

"Remember Marty and Alan? The basketball players?" Kevin remembers: two giants who drank cocktails by the pitcher, but couldn't dance. They were famous in Portugal. "I promised I'd call once I got back to the States."

"So you wanna call them now?"

"Don't worry, I have a card." She enters numbers into his cordless. "Hey!" she screams, sliding a photograph from her wallet and tapping it. Two black men in warm-up suits— towering above a VW Bug—smile back.

Michelle wants to shop. Kevin usually hates the mall, but today, waiting outside Victoria's Secret, he's enjoying himself. Michelle drifts in and out of his vision, gliding among satin teddies and furry bras. Could he live a life where he often waited like this, on a bench in a mall, for the woman he loved? His last girlfriend, Hannah, was kind of a slob—cut-off sweat-shirts, baseball caps, flip-flops. Michelle, though, has style: to know it and be moved by it. She comes out of the store toting two swollen paper bags. She bites her lip. She looks giddy.

"So," Kevin asks, "what's the damage?"

"You'll die," she says.

"Tell me."

"Four hundred," she replies. "I put it on my mom's credit card. She's gonna kill me. I can't believe I just did that. I already have, like, a huge bill."

"Like, how much?" he asks.

She scrunches up her nose. "Like ten thousand dollars?"

That night Kevin and Michelle eat spaghetti on the couch, drinking wine and watching bad Friday-night television. Michelle insists on washing the dishes. Then she plops down beside him, leans her head on his shoulder.

"Tired?" he asks.

"I could go night-night."

"Want me to make up the couch?"

She pouts. "Can't I snuggle with you?"

In a twin bed, they don't have much of a choice. They snuggle. They talk. They kiss. It's nice. They touch. Michelle's skin is buttery smooth, but her body's mushy, like those squishy gel-filled oblongs—water snakes, they're called—that fly from your hand when you squeeze them. During underwear removal, Kevin nearly falls off the bed. It takes so long to get going, he wonders if it'll go at all. Finally, there's penetration. Then something goes wrong. Not for him. For her. At least it looks that way. Her face keeps contracting. Then he can't help it: he's wilting.

Neither Kevin nor Michelle utters a word. Kevin lays his head against her chest. The thump of her heart fills his head; he wonders if his is beating as fast. He's afraid to move, afraid to look this girl in the face, so he lies there until she gets out of bed and walks out of the room.

"Michelle?" he calls. He stumbles down the hall in the dark. She's on the porch, a cigarette between her fingers.

"What's wrong?" he asks.

She sniffles, rubs one of her eyes. "I'm sorry," she says. "This… this is what happens when I make love, okay?"

"What do you mean?"

"I mean this," she says, waving a hand in front of her glistening face. "I cry. I don't know why. It just happens. I'll be fine in a minute."

He nods. The streetlamps have frosted the pines. He wants to say something. He wants to help. He says, "I didn't know you smoked."

She shrugs. "They were out here."

He lights one.

"Listen," she says. "There are some other things you should know about me."

Her father, the one she told him about, the one who flies planes out of Napa Valley for the rich and famous, and has seen the homes of Francis Ford Coppola and Jack Nicholson, is not her father. Her mother, the woman whose credit card she carries, is not her mother. Her real mother is her aunt. This aunt who is not her aunt but her real mother is crazy, some kind of schizo who tried to burn down her house with Michelle and Michelle's brother inside. That's not all. She binge drinks. She spends money she doesn't have. She throws her food up after she eats; she's already done this twice since she arrived.

"Still like me?" she says, and smirks. She taps the cigarette. The coal tumbles into the dark.

"Of course," he says. He wants to help, to relate, but his only regret is that nothing all that bad has ever happened to him—so he has no excuse when a crazy girl stumbles into his world and he fucks her incompetently, then fails to comfort her when she cries. He has no dead mother, no abusive father, no history of drug addiction. What he got was love, unconditionally. He got dog-loyal parents. If, in some alternate reality, he tried to kill them and failed, they would lick at their wounds and crawl back, as though he had been wronged and they were the ones who had failed him.

In ten minutes, Michelle's snoring in bed. Kevin can't sleep. He thinks about the Dog Den, wonders how many dogs are up, if any can't sleep, or if they bark in their dreams. He thinks about Francine, the Most Important Dog at the lab, the one worth most to the scientists. She lives in a tiny cage with wheels. Francine's special because her meds have upped her clotting time by a thousandth of a second. When she runs in the gravel courtyard, her body (curved because of the smallness of her cage, which is stainless steel so she won't injure herself) goes in circles. He's noted the look on her face: pure stupid doggy joy. The messed-up thing? She can't wait to get into her cage.

The next morning, over bowls of Cheerios with sliced bananas, Michelle's cheerfulness seems to have been recharged.

"So," she asks, "how many girls have you slept with?"

"Very few. Why?"

"Just wondering. Do you usually not wear a condom?"

"No. I mean yes."

"So last night?"

"I don't know." Kevin's heart races. He remembers Gary, who claims to have slept with eighty-some women, not once donning a prophylactic. He tells himself he's not that guy. He believes in the spread of disease.

"I don't have anything to worry about, right?"

"No," he says. "Do I?"

"Nope," she says. She takes a big spoonful of cereal. She looks around the room as she chews. Her eyes widen. "I just realized what this place needs."

"What's that?"

"A dog! What? Don't you like dogs?"

"Sure, I like dogs fine."

"Then let's get you one," she says. Hand on his arm, her thumb strokes his skin, like a real girlfriend's thumb would. "To remind you of me when I leave."

Kevin doesn't want a dog. He's not even sure if his lease permits it. But Michelle wants him to have one. Maybe she assumes a dog will improve the quality of his life, and that if she leaves him with a dog, the weekend won't be an utter failure. Whatever it is, he doesn't want to disappoint her. Even though he wants to, he can't bring himself to say no.

Adopting a golden retriever puppy at the Orange County Animal Shelter costs ninety nonrefundable dollars. Kevin has ninety dollars, but it's all been dedicated to utilities. Still, he writes Ninety dollars on a check and hands it to a smiling fat woman. He drives to the mall, buys a bowl and a pillow and a leash and a housebreaking guide and a bag of food. He charges it.

"Don't you just love him?" Michelle asks. The dog licks her mouth.

"I do," Kevin says. He remembers the puppy cage at the Blood Lab, the dirtiest cage in the whole place. Floors smeared with shit. Shit in their puppy fur, shit in their puppy ears. They leap all over him, leaving tiny shit prints on his pants. They are, in a word, vile—at least until baths restore their cuteness. It seems futile, and yet generous, that they get bathed at all. Keisha does them one at a time and wraps them in towels afterwards like little squirmy burritos. She holds them as long as she can, as if savoring what it's like for each one to be clean.

Michelle wants to celebrate the dog-getting at her favorite restaurant: the Olive Garden. As the training manual suggested, Kevin locked the dog in the bathroom: This closed dim space, the book claimed, will provide a comfortably familiar, den-like condition. Dinner's Michelle's treat. She'll put everything on her mom's Visa: what difference will another hundred dollars make? Kevin raises a glass of wine to that. They eat pasta and salad and tiramisu. Michelle visits the bathroom; Kevin wonders if she plans to puke it all up. He doesn't care. He's a half-drunk dog owner dining with a beautiful woman who will leave him tomorrow. As he's downing the last of his wine, the waiter delivers the bill: Michelle's mom's Visa has been declined. Kevin accompanies the waiter to the register, instructs him to run his card. When Michelle returns, he hands over her Visa, tells her he signed her name, left a cash tip. She buys it. At the car, he unlocks her side first. She kisses him. She tastes like toothpaste and garlic. Kevin wants this to last. Finally, something real is happening, something meaningful enough to be sad.

That night they walk the dog around the lawns of Ramsgate, beneath the pines, past buildings whose living rooms sputter with TV light. Michelle can't believe she's leaving tomorrow. Kevin can't believe he has to get back to work. "So yeah," Michelle says, "what's this mysterious lab job, anyway?" Kevin takes a deep breath. He describes the people who work there; he explains, as best he can, the freebleeder situation. He tells a story: One day, the shih tzus, which share a cage, managed to grab the paw of the dog in the neighboring cage, a Great Dane named Monty, a heart-breakingly bashful dog Kevin often finds cowering in some corner. The dogs started fighting, trying to bite each other through the wire mesh, so Kevin went into Monty's cage and took the squeegee stick and poked at them, screaming, "Cut it out," but nothing happens, so Kevin, genius that he is, stuck his foot in between Monty and the shih tzus. Well, Monty, sweet, meek, mellow Monty—the dog Kevin's spent hours sweet-talking just so he can pat his huge, trembling head—chomped down on his boot. Kevin leaped onto the wire wall. He kicked and screamed, but Monty held on, his teeth sinking deeper into Kevin's boot. Eventually the dog let go. Kevin couldn't believe it. Monty's teeth had pierced the rubber, penetrated his skin.

Michelle frowns. The dog chews on her fingers. She acts like it doesn't hurt.

"How," she asks, "can you work there?"

Kevin shrugs. "Somebody has to do it."

"Why?"

"They don't have anywhere else to go."

"No, I mean, why do they have to, I don't know, use animals?"

"I guess because they can't use people."

"Well," Michelle says, "I couldn't do it."

Kevin nods. He's not sure he can, either.

At the airport, Michelle kisses him good-bye, promises to call and write and send pictures. "I had such a good time," she says. "Take good care of Eliot." She means the dog.

"I will," Kevin says.

"Don't look so sad," she says. "I'll be back." Kevin nods. He knows he'll never see her again.

Back home, Kevin presses the dog's little face against a chewed up couch cushion, a torn book, a gnawed-on chair leg, and two wet spots on the carpet, telling him no, no, no. He doesn't like doing this, but he remembers hearing that it was the thing to do.

Kevin wants to give up, drive Eliot back to the shelter. Instead, he breaks open a film canister with two green buds inside, smashes one into his pipe, and fires it up. The dog leaps into his lap. What the hell, he thinks. Maybe the dog just needs to relax. He holds the dog in his arms and blows smoke into its face.

The dog looked fine before he went to bed, but when Kevin wakes up to pee, it's not okay. Its eyelids are heavy, its head trembles. It tries to walk. It wobbles, falls. It whines. He slides a hand beneath the dog's plump little belly; its chest heaves as though it can't get enough air. Its pulse beats against his fingertips, and a tingling—as though tiny molecules are passing from the dog's body to Kevin's—enlivens his hands, his arms, his chest. Kevin's once-sluggish heart thumps wildly, as if to relay this urgent, obvious message: Do something. But what? What do you do for a drugged up dog? He can't call the vet, not at this hour, not for this: he's terrified of losing the dog, but he doesn't want to have to say what he did. There's nothing to do except bring the dog into bed, press his lips to its fur, and ask him to please not die.

The next morning, Kevin considers calling in sick. The dog has survived, seems totally okay now, but he feels guilty about leaving him in the bathroom all day. He lets him chew on his finger, but his teeth are too sharp. He tosses him a rubber ducky and closes the door. He calls Michelle to see if she made it back okay. He gets her voice mail, hangs up after the beep.

At the lab, Robin's making new time cards. Keisha's poking a bloodhound named Mayberry with a butterfly needle, and Brad's hosing out the Pig Palace. In the Dog Den, it's the familiar sound of fifty-odd dogs barking, excited to see him. Kevin unravels the hose, walks to the end to spray out the puppy cage. He always starts and ends with the puppy cage. It gets dirty fast enough to do twice. But today the puppies are gone, and their cage—an empty rectangle of concrete—is clean.

The kennel door creaks open. It's Robin, leading Mayberry back to his cage.

"Where are the puppies?" Kevin asks.

She frowns. "Didn't you know? They were euthanized last week."

"Why?"

Robin shakes her head. "We just didn't have the room."

Kevin drops the hose, steps into the cage, and swings the door closed. He squats, hooks a finger around a rung of wire to steady himself. In the next cage, a blind beagle named Harvey licks as much of his hand as he can. In the cages beyond his, Kevin watches Monty and Mayberry and Tomata and Dorcas. They pace. They jump against the wire. Their tails slap piss puddles. They cock their heads, anticipating his next move. They want their heads patted. They want to hump his leg. They want to run the lane while he cleans. And Kevin wants them to enjoy these things. He does. In the end, though, he does what's easiest: he exits the puppy cage and heads for the door, refusing to look a single dog in the face. He feels like he's failed them somehow, that he should've found some way to relieve them of their wretched lives. But there's no rescuing these animals. They have no idea they even need to be saved.

STRAIGHTEDGE

When my ex-wife, Lauren—wearing a short, smart haircut, a pair of state trooper style Ray-Bans, a man's red Polo shirt and khaki shorts—met me at the Atlanta airport and I saw my son's face in a transparent rectangle dangling from the Land Rover's rear view, I hardly recognized him. His head was bald—a smudgy gray, as if someone had erased his hair, but forgotten to blow off the dust—and he was making an X with his index fingers.

"Straightedge," Lauren explained. I watched her arms— the lean tendons flexing—as she opened a plump wallet and slid out a bill for the parking attendant. When she accelerated, a sack of dried flowers tumbled off an ottoman on the backseat.

"Straightedge?" I asked.

She nodded. "For two years now. Doesn't smoke, doesn't drink, doesn't take drugs, doesn't eat meat, doesn't cuss, doesn't have sex. Skates all day and night." When a ligament in her neck flared, my throat constricted. Lauren's body— browned and slender and velvety—had flourished. Mine, unfortunately, could not compare. My flesh had paled in the sputtering light of casinos and the dashboard of the Greyhound bus, which, for the last decade, I'd been driving from L.A. to Las Vegas. Even now, as the Rover thumped along a stretch of uneven freeway, I could feel my love handles quiver.

"How do you sleep?" I asked.

"Huh?"

"With the ramp or whatever? The half-pike?"

"Half-pipe. It's downstairs with the pool. Steve finally drained it for him last summer. We're three flights up. Ian could blow himself up and we probably wouldn't hear it."

Ian Hart. My son. You might have heard of him. He won a bronze medal last summer; he was only sixteen. His last name used to be Traechler, like mine. But after Lauren asked me to leave, and after Steve Hart—generous, savvy, classy Steve, with the kind of smile only an oral surgeon can own—materialized, it made sense to acquire a new name, especially if it assured one a place in the headlines: The Kid's Got Hart. All Hart. Lion-Harted. Etc.

It hurt. But I couldn't blame him.

The night before the games, at the Kudzu Café, I told Ian I'd seen Bobby Sherman shoot a three pointer in the same arena—the Omni—where Ian would attempt the 720 Upside-Down Cake. State Championship, 1980. Five years before he was born. "I once witnessed a champion there," I said, to instill what sense of legacy I could. "Isn't that ironic?"

"That's not ironic," Ian corrected, sipping ice water. "It's coincidental."

We had a tradition, my son and I—if twice counts as tradition, which, at the time, I thought it did. The tradition was that I took Ian out to dinner and insisted he order as much of whatever as he wanted, which was never all that much because he'd learned to direct his appetite in more beneficial directions. At the end of the meal, I would give him a hundred-dollar bill, an act of generosity I could not really afford, but upon which I would insist, even if, like last time (when, get this, the kid was only twelve), Ian managed to sneak it into my back pocket.

I ordered a Heineken and a Scotch, both of which I sipped alternately between puffs of a Marlboro Light, careful to place the glass ashtray on an empty chair beside me and blow the smoke out of the corner of my mouth, so as not to contaminate the athlete.

"So," I began. "Do you have a girlfriend?"

"Nope," Ian replied. He wore a black shirt with three-quarter-length sleeves and a logo that said sXe. A fresh scrape on his wrist glistened. "What about you?"

"I've been seeing someone," I said.

I'd met Portia a few months before, in the laundry room of the hotel where I lived—a place I despised so much that I went only once a month, toting my thirty pairs of underwear, thirty pairs of socks, thirty undershirts, and the four tropical shirts and black shorts I saved for weekends (Greyhound laundered my uniform). I'd been there most of the morning, reading a five-year-old copy of People I'd found curled behind one of the dryers, so I wouldn't have to make eye contact with a hooded boy in a Raiders parka, who was twisting a Rubik's Cube while his whites dried. When Portia entered, she was wearing pink knee-high boots, a tiger-print skirt, a yellow jacket made of plastic, and a long blond wig. She was looking for Room Z. I said there wasn't any such place. She unwrapped a cube of gum, placed it on her tongue, and asked if there was anything she could do for me. At the time, I'd thought she was a man—a very tall, exquisitely featured black man. I said, "No thank you." She persisted. She let me investigate what she was offering. I told her I was only interested in her mouth and that I no longer bothered with prophylactics. The boy with the Rubik's Cube whistled. Portia said, "Whatever." I asked her how much. "Fifty," she said. I said I'd pay her ten and we went up to my room.

After that, Monday nights belonged to Portia and me. I'd order Mongolian Beef with extra fortune cookies, and by the time she finished doing her thing, the Happy China guy would arrive. We'd eat, watch Fear Factor—"no they didn't," she'd always say, when couples stuffed live worms in their mouths—then she'd leave, and I'd lie in bed, trying not to think about where she went next. Once, she stayed for the entire night, which was extra, but worth it, because she told me the story of her family: how her father, one of Marlon Brando's personal chefs, had acquired psychic powers after surviving an auto accident, and how, on the eve of the first moon walk, he'd dreamed of her mother, a Spanish salsa dancer; they'd met the next day in a posh Beverly Hills market, where her father was purchasing Chilean sea bass for Brando. I didn't believe a word of it, but I loved her voice— a husky, articulate drawl—and as long as I lifted tiny, inspirational spoons of blow to her nose she kept going.

"What about sex?" I asked Ian. "Is it true you refuse it?"

He chuckled. "Yeah," he said. He rested a Converse All Star on his knee, peeled a sliver of battered rubber from the edge. "But it's not like I'm turning down a whole lot of propositions."

"Are you gay?" I whispered. "Because you can tell me if—"

"What does being gay have to do with it? Don't gay people do it?"

"Of course they do. Everyone does. Everyone except you."

"Listen," Ian said, settling back in his chair, hands folded in front of his face. One thing I loved about my son: he always indulged my little interviews. "I just think it clouds your mind. It's like a drug. Which, no offense," he added, nodding toward my end of the table, "I totally avoid. I have friends who are, like, addicted to sex. When they want it, they like hop around and twitch and say stuff like, 'Man I gotta get laid.'"

I dragged on my cigarette, pondering my next question, which I'd meant to lead up to but now blurted out. "How often do you think about the fact that your father, your real, biological father, is a failure?"

Ian laughed, then coughed, waving a hand to clear the smoke that, despite my best efforts, had drifted into his face. "You're not a failure," he said. His eyes watered. "You've just made some questionable decisions."

"Ian. I live in a motel. I drive a Greyhound bus from Los Angeles to Las Vegas six times a week. I transport people like myself to a place where they can be at their worst."

"You sound like you might enjoy it."

"Maybe I do."

Ian shook his head. "You're here now, aren't you?"

"I'm too late. I might as well be an ex-father."

"Surely there must be something," Ian said, his cheeks bulging as he chomped a bite of vegan burrito, "that makes you happy to be you."

I told him then what he probably already knew: that every Saturday morning for the past fifteen years, I'd got up and told myself I wouldn't gamble, and in my mind I'd think, This is it, this would be the Saturday I wouldn't lose any money. But then after breakfast—one plate of steak and eggs with black coffee at the diner down the street from my motel—I'd say to myself, Let's just see what's happening at Marty's, and the next thing I knew I'd be setting down a dangerous amount money on a horse that I had picked not because of the odds, or because I thought the horse was the best horse, or because the horse had been sired by a champion, but because the whole thing, the act of choosing this horse, was completely random, and putting all my money on something completely random was the only thing at that moment which would excite me.

Ian ran a hand over his head. "So," he murmured, "how much money have you lost? Like, over your lifetime."

"You wouldn't want to know."

"Yeah I would."

I told him how much. There was a slight pause. Then he laughed. I laughed with him. The number, after all, was absurd.

Steve Hart—oral surgeon, onetime competitive bass fisherman, and doting husband to my ex-wife—had won millions playing the stock market. The morning before the games, he showed me a software package that, using some ancient Asian candlestick method, could predict winners.

"I have no interest in any of this," I said, but Steve kept clicking through the charts. "I'm telling you, I won't remember anything you've said in five seconds."

"I don't get it," Steve replied, stroking his moustache. "You're a gambler."

I tried to explain that there wasn't any science to my gambling—that you couldn't confront chaos with candlesticks. You could use only your bare, tingling flesh and a fistful of cash, hoping that, as you relinquished everything, you would hit the jackpot.

It happens; every dedicated gambler hits the jackpot at least once. I spent my twenty grand on ecstasy, two young blondes I'd found grinding against each other in a club in South Beach, and room service. At the time it felt glorious— the freedom of transgression, the kind of stupefying pleasure that inches you closer toward death, no matter how many condoms you're wearing—but then, when it was over, when the money had been blown, I was gripping the hot plastic wheel of a Greyhound, barreling toward Sin City, where, at the feet of Chance, I yearned to worship again.

"What should I wear?" I asked. I was sipping a mimosa in one of Steve's old robes while Lauren ran a sponge along the polished length of a spigot in the Hart kitchen, where she'd prepared Ian's favorite pregame breakfast: vegan waffles, fresh strawberries, and soy bacon. Now, she and I were the only ones left in a room strewn with syrupy plates. I tried to imagine it as ours, but with that boyish haircut and that sleeveless white blouse showcasing her naked arms, I barely recognized her. She had style now, and money, and it was hard to think of her as the old Lauren, and therefore difficult to concoct, using her current body, a fantasy I could believe.

"For God's sake, Roger," she said. She swiped her brow with a wrist, leaving a faint stripe of moisture behind. "It's a sporting event. Wear whatever."

"I was just checking. I don't want to stand out."

"You'll look fine," she replied.

I fortified my cocktail with a splash of vodka. "I want to thank you again for the hospitality," I said.

"You know you're welcome here anytime."

"Maybe I'll move in," I joked.

"Right." She shook her head and chuckled. "That'd work out great."

"Let me ask you a question," I said. "Purely hypothetical. Let's say, and this would be tragic, of course, but what if Steve, what if something should happen to him?"

"What do you mean?" she asked.

"Would all this be ours?"

She smirked at me, then capped the Absolut.

I set down the champagne flute, picked up a mug I assumed had been mine, and walked south, out of the kitchen. I wandered through a maze of rooms, sipping cold java. I saw a wall of antelope antlers. I saw a great gleaming table upon which sat a vase of brilliant, frothy rods. I saw a cabinet thingy whose paint was peeling. I saw the head of a tusked beast. I saw a terrace of rare plants in a room of glass. I searched for but did not find, Ian, Lauren, Steve, and myself upon a wall of photographs of people I did not recognize. The house was a vast collection of things I could not name, an anthology of symbols beyond my reach.

At the games—in an arena pulsing with light and people and alternative rock—I felt rejuvenated: I had a pair of Lauren's underwear stuffed down the front of my pants. Back when I was exploring the cavernous depths of the Hart home, I'd ended up in a closet I'd assumed was hers. When I'd found the underwear in a laundry basket, I'd smashed the cloth against my nose, hoping the tang would transport me. Unfortunately, the fabric was odorless. I'd heard someone coming and shoved the briefs into my pants. They felt good, a little lumpy but good, so even after Lauren passed the walk-in, where I was hiding between a sequined jacket and a leather pantsuit, I left them there. Maybe, I thought, they'll bring us good luck during the games.

Despite my high spirits, I couldn't watch Ian live during the prelims: only the JumboTron replays. If I watched him in real time, I told myself, he'd flub up. It was okay, though. This was the big one, the X Games, and there were plenty of other things to admire. The lights. The other skaters. The rapt audience. The cameramen. The flashbulbs. The reporters. The scantily clad. The pierced. The tattooed. The infants. My ex-wife. My ex-wife's husband, the hugely successful and charming Steve Hart, whom I often wished I could comfortably hug.

When they announced Ian's name, Lauren grabbed my hand. This is it, I thought, because it reminded me of the long ago times when we held each other's hands—when we held each other's bodies. I knew there was no it, never would be an it again, but still, it felt good to hold her hand, to feel her holding my hand, to hold on to the feeling which was happening now of holding this woman-who-used-to-be-my-wife's hand. To pretend that we were united as we watched the person whose bones and tissues had formed inside her, a person who would risk the same bones and tissues under hot arena lights. To pretend that after this was over, I could return to a life that might have been mine.

I was the one who cheated. I hadn't been caught. I had gambled, but not with getting caught; I was king of not getting caught. But I wasn't king of my own secrets, and in the end, it was my conscience that failed me. It was laying in bed thinking about what I had done with another woman as my month-old son lay on my chest, his warm, sticky, stuttering breath snapping in and out of his new lungs—his arms and legs squirming suddenly when he startled. It was his small, impossibly delicate body rising and falling on my own rising and falling body which was fevered with lies. It was the impulse to purge myself of my sins, which I did, and from which I would not recover.

Everyone knew every contestant deserved to win—you could tell by the compassion in the eyes of the audience. Those kids, they'd all suffered. They'd all torn flaps of skin from their elbows and knees, they'd all viewed their own splintered bones poking through shimmering fat, they'd all sacrificed young, supple bodies that would never be the same. But only one story could end untragically. Only one could win.

Before Ian, a Japanese kid named Jimmy Lee had taken first when he scored a 9.3. His father, sporting a beige Members Only jacket and square, silver-framed glasses, sat three rows down from us, squinting through a video camera that resembled a high-tech cannon. I wondered, as this father's machine followed the parabolas of his son, if his son even existed. If maybe his son, so skinny and so dorky in the way only a kid with glasses not unlike his father's and an oversize helmet could be, was merely a fantastic hologram, projected by the cannon. That might've explained his greatness. He'd caught some fairly large and improbable air.

One thing was clear, however. My son was better. I know all fathers think this but it was different with Ian. Today he would try something that nobody else had ever dared: The 720 Upside-Down Cake.

And I was there. I had made it. I had come to visit my son and his family and cheer him to victory.

He was leading up to it, swishing back and forth on the ramp with nonchalance, with the kind of ease that allowed us—the friends, the fans, the parents—to feel confident. He was in control.

I told myself not to look, that if I looked he would fail. But then, there he was—in the air. He was turning and turning and I was turning and the world was turning and the flashbulbs exploded like lightning and my son and I for a moment were Gods, as the camera was on him and the camera was on me and my giant face was on some giant TV monitor because I was the father and I knew we were going to make it, and that what would come after—the promotions, the invitations, the endorsements, the success—would arrive like a windfall to drown us. I knew this in my heart, so I whooped. I whooped louder than I've ever whooped. The whoop burned like a coal in my throat. The whoop rang out like a bell across the semisilent, awed, anticipatory crowd.

When his head hit first, I knew he was dead. He laid there, eyes closed. Finally, he moved. He moaned. He punched the ramp with his fist. I predicted paramedics and a gurney. He would never skate again.

Then, miraculously, he leaped up. He waved but did not smile. Everyone was clapping because he had tried it and lived. Everyone was clapping because he was jogging away from what could have been death. Lauren let go of my hand to clap and when the clapping was over her hand was gone.

If it hadn't been for Portia, I might've been a no-show at the games. Three weeks before, I'd persuaded her to stay long enough to share a bottle of Jameson I'd bought after a horse named Peasant's Fancy had taken second at Churchill Downs. The wigless, cornrowed Portia wore a pink tube top and Levi's, and her chipped toenails had been slathered with fuchsia. I was staring at her mouth, which I loved not just because of how it made me feel, but because her overbite had imprinted two tiny slits into her bottom lip, and at the time, I could imagine nothing more beautiful.

"If you don't go," she said, staring at the TV, where a woman in a glass box weathered a deluge of slugs, "you'll regret it." Against my advice, she'd flooded her glass of Jameson with Diet Pepsi; every time she took a sip she winced.

"But what if Ian regrets the fact that I'm coming? I'm not a good person to have at high-pressure events. I'm not lucky."

"That's cute," Portia said. She smiled, flashing her silver eyetooth, and placed a ringed hand against her breast. "My boy actually believes in luck."

The night after the games, my last in Atlanta before I returned to the desert, Steve drove us to Buckhead, where he bought us dinner at a fancy restaurant with white tablecloths. Every few minutes, thin waiters appeared and used sharp plastic thingies to shave the crumbs that fell from our lips and off the table. Steve said to get anything—no holds barred—and in the end he bought me one green salad, one rare steak sandwich, five asparagus spears, four Scotches and two Heinekens. Sadly, it wasn't enough to deliver me to the place I'd hoped to go, though it was enough to encourage me to squeeze Lauren's leg while announcing that I was still in love with her and always would be.

"Roger, please," she murmured, swirling her chardonnay. "This isn't the time."

"I have to say these things now," I said. "Soon I'll be gone."

"I'll go ahead and track down that bill," Steve said, wrinkling his nose.

"Well," Lauren said, raising her eyebrows and smoothing the front of her white blouse. "I guess I'll make a trip to the little girl's room."

When they were gone, I turned to Ian, who'd eaten only a fruit smoothie that he'd smuggled into the restaurant, and a quarter of his tomato-bean polenta. He stabbed the sludge thoughtfully with his fork. He had not spoken to—had not looked at—anyone. Which was okay. It was obvious he was meditating on his loss.

"So," I asked, "how does it feel?"

"To lose?" He pinched the tablecloth, making a tiny ramp out of the fabric.

"The fall. Was it as bad as it looked?"

"Nah," he said, a lilt in his voice as though the pain had just occurred to him. "The actual physical pain, that's like the least of it."

"You know," I said, grinning as I sucked a Scotch-coated ice cube. "Maybe you should've had a couple drinks before the games. You know, a shot or two to limber you up."

"Yeah," Ian replied. "You're probably right. I mean, look at what it's done for you." I wanted to laugh. It was a good one. But Ian wasn't smiling.

That night, in the room to which I'd been assigned for the weekend—a room with a trickling fountain and plants with leathery, bladelike leaves—I couldn't sleep. I was thinking about Portia. I wondered if the underwear would fit her. I wondered if they would fit me. I wadded them up and put them in my mouth. As I chomped their silky bulk, I calculated the cost of getting home—drinks in the airport, drinks on the plane, a few dollars to throw toward a ticket writer at Bally's—and realized I had come up short. I checked my wallet. I only had two fives.

Ian was in his room, sleeping. In the stripe of light that fell from the hallway, I could see pages from skateboarding magazines tacked to the wall, along with a poster of an emaciated kid screaming into a microphone, the cord of which he'd wrapped around his arm like a makeshift tourniquet. I spotted the jeans Ian had worn to dinner that night, and picked them up off the floor. The pockets were empty, except for a few pennies. Then I saw it: the hundred I'd given him laid on his desk, beneath a water glass. I lifted the glass and slid the bill into my hand.

"Dad?" Ian said. I froze.

"Yes, Son?"

"What are you doing?"

I swallowed. My mouth was dry, my armpits moistening. "I couldn't sleep. I wondered if you were up." I crushed the bill in my fist. "I wondered if maybe you wanted to talk."

Ian flicked on a lamp. He shielded his eyes. "Talk? Now?"

"Actually," I said, "I came to apologize."

"For what?"

"You're going to think I'm crazy."

He yawned. "Dad," he said, "I already think you're crazy."

"Okay," I said. "Here's the thing. Before the games, I made a bet with myself."

"You bet on the games?"

"Just in my mind." I sat down on the bed and landed on his foot. He slid it slowly out from under me. "I told myself not to look. I knew if I looked you wouldn't make it." I stared at his puzzled face—the side he'd fallen on—at what looked like a swollen pouch of fluid. I watched his mouth—the thin angled lips, I realized, were mine.

"What I'm trying to tell you," I said, "is that it's my fault that you lost."

Ian rubbed his eyes. He squinted at his clock. "Dad," he said, "it's late."

He was right. It was late.

"Listen," he said, rising to a sitting position. "It's okay. Let's just sleep on it now, though, okay?"

He held out his hand for me to shake. I took his right hand with my right hand and squeezed. When I did, Ian yanked me forward and embraced me. I hugged him back and patted his back with my left fist, where the hundred had grown moist.

"I'm going to make some changes when I get back," I told him.

"Good. You should."

"You inspired me," I said. "I may even go straightedge. Give up everything."

After I said it, the lie almost seemed possible. I envisioned myself in a tear-shaped helmet and biker shorts, pedaling through the desert. I'd sweat away the pounds. I'd live off egg whites, bananas, and turkey sandwiches. The next time I showed up, I'd have tanned, bladelike calves and thousands of miles under my belt.

"Dad?" Ian asked.

"Yeah?"

"That actually kind of hurts."

"Sorry," I said. But I didn't let go. Not right away. I didn't know when I'd see my son again, and figured I should say something important, leave him with some kind of fatherly wisdom he could chew on in the years ahead. Unfortunately, I'd run out of fatherly wisdom a long time ago, and nothing I could think of—You can do it. You're tops. I love you— sounded like me, so I just squeezed him again and let the crumpled hundred in my hand float to the floor, hoping that when he found it he might think of me.

STEWARDS OF THE EARTH

Jennifer Husk had no intention of attending North Atlantic College; she'd sent her application just to see if she was smart enough to go. Despite the fact that she'd refused to include the fifty-dollar application fee, a letter of acceptance had arrived two months later, with a handbook explaining the school's no-tolerance position on alcohol, tobacco, drugs, rock music, and "flesh food" (i.e., meat of any kind). She also received a course catalog whose cover featured four portraits: a black guy in a rugby shirt contemplating a globe; an Asian girl spinning a basketball on an index finger; a tuxedoed Indian boy straddling a cello; and a freckle-faced girl folding her hands over an open Bible. Below these pictures, a caption appeared: Success begins in the soul. These people, Jen reminded herself, believed they had souls; they took classes with names like Light Bearers to the Remnant, Gift of Prophecy and Life in the Balance. Also, Jen guessed, they had to have money: scholarships, loans, trust funds, savings bonds, something. How else could they afford to pay the twenty-eight-thousand-dollar tuition? Jen had nothing, aside from the notion that doors, if they were supposed to be opened, would be opened. The tuition deadline approached. Scratch-offs and Powerball tickets failed to deliver; nobody died and bequeathed her an estate. The deadline passed. Jen tossed out the catalog. Obviously, it wasn't meant to be. The first day of class came and went. Then the second. The third. The fourth. On the fifth day of the semester, she made a decision: she would go anyway.

Intro to Humanities met in the committee room of the White

House, a sprawling Victorian mansion whose bedrooms had been converted into classrooms. The room, with its scarlet wallpaper, crystal chandelier and table of shellacked wood, was a place where rich people had once taken their meals. Now a plump, stooped woman with round cheeks and a gray bowl cut sat at the head of this table, fiddling with a slide projector. Laycock, Jen thought. Leetha Laverne Laycock. Jen had checked out Laycock's personal webpage. She knew Laycock had a B.A. from North Atlantic, an M.A. from Assumption College, a PhD. from Holy Cross. In her faculty photo, Laycock resembled a good-natured, toothy mammal: a burrower that made homey nests underground. In person? Laycock looked the same—only older.

Once class began, Laycock dimmed the lights; her projector flung the image of a painting onto the wall. In the painting a woman danced before a floating, disembodied head. Strings of blood streamed from its neck. The head, emanating saw blades of light, showed no signs of missing its body. It gazed unapologetically at the dancer, who was clothed in jeweled garters and flowing scarves. Jen's cheeks flooded with warmth. She was not, she guessed, supposed to find the image arousing.

"The Apparition," Laycock said. "Gustave Moreau. Nineteenth Century." Every few seconds, her eyebrows jerked backwards. "Anyone remember Salome?" she asked. "The harlot who danced for King Herod? He enjoyed the dancing so much he offered her half his kingdom. But Salome didn't want half his kingdom. She wanted the head of John the Baptist on a platter. Why would someone want a head instead of a kingdom?"

A puffy-faced girl, her cheeks perforated with acne scars, raised her hand. "Maybe," she said, "this Salome person was power hungry."

Laycock giggled silently. She pointed to a young man wearing an orange warm-up suit and a bright white hat upon which the letters N and Y sparkled. He scooted his chair back, then stood. "Obviously," he said, "Salome is a ho, right? No disrespect, but for real. Look at her. Ya'll know how ho's be trippin'."

A few students chuckled. Laycock, it seemed, couldn't wipe the grin off her face. She also didn't seem to have any answers, didn't seem to mind that nobody did. "Nicely put," she'd say, as the theories piled up. "Very reasonable."

Maybe, Jen thought, Paul was right: college was for chumps.

The next morning, the head of John the Baptist appeared to Jen in a dream. The head—bearded and bleeding and beset with pupil-less eyes—rotated slowly, clicking. At first, Jen couldn't make out what the head was saying. Then she realized: it wasn't saying anything. It was singing that Carpenters song about birds appearing: just like me/ they long to be/ close to you. In the middle of the song, she woke up.

Paul straddled a corner of their futon. He held a Fisher-Price Movie Viewer to his left eye. He'd received the viewer in the mail the day before, along with a cardboard box of yellow, rectangular cartridges. He slid a cartridge into the viewer, looked through a tiny hole, and spun a red handle on the side. Clickety-clack. A soundless movie (he had Mickey Mouse, Big Bird, Pink Panther, and Bugs Bunny) played as fast as he could spin the handle, forward or backward.

"You're gonna be late," Jen said, glancing at the clock. It was ten to nine. Paul wore a T-shirt with a Wolverine decal, a pair of crud-streaked jeans. Every day, he packed two

Baloney sandwiches on white bread into a rusted lunch box, and drove his Honda Civic to Framingham, where he cashiered at a bookstore.

"You're the one who hasn't gotten out of bed," he said. "Don't you have school today?"

"It's called college," Jen said. "And it's not until later."

"Must be nice to get paid to sit around and read."

"I'm not getting paid," Jen said.

"Your tuition's free, isn't it?"

It was. Sort of. Someone was paying the teachers to show up and teach. A lot of someones. Only none of them was her. She hadn't explained this to Paul, who, after dropping out of Fitchburg State after two semesters with a 1.6 GPA, had taken issue with higher education. Instead, she'd told him the school had given her a full ride. He could not, she'd thought, argue with a full ride. And he hadn't. "Congratulations," he'd said. "Now you can waste your time for free."

Paul slid the cartridge from the movie viewer, returned it to the blister pack he'd carefully opened using a straight razor. "You seen my Wish Book?"

"Wish Book?"

"You know. My Sears catalog. The one from 1985? I can't find it."

"Maybe it's a sign," Jen said. "You've used up all your wishes."

"Don't act dumb," Paul said. "Seriously. That thing cost me ten bucks on eBay."

Another reason Paul didn't need college? He was starting a business—an online venture that depended upon his ability to track down obscure relics from his childhood and resell them at inflated prices. He'd recently paid fifty bucks for a stuffed bear that moved its mouth when you slid a cassette into its back. According to Paul, he could get a hundred bucks for that bear, easy. In ten years? A thousand.

Paul went to work; Jen yanked the covers over her head. She closed her eyes. The head reappeared. The whites of its eyes were slick as boiled eggs; the lids, lined with dried blood, flickered. Coiled clumps of hair writhed of their own volition. Its lips, blistered, quivered and drooled.

Enough, Jen thought. She got up. She made the bed. She picked up the boxers Paul had left on the floor. She folded the Scrabble board they'd abandoned the night before, sweeping the words they'd made—dark, mend, war, fauna— into a velvety pouch. She lifted the futon mattress, retrieved Paul's Wish Book. Walking downstairs, she flipped through the kid section, noting little boys in Popeye pajamas, a Rocky Balboa punching bag. Paul's birthday was coming up: no doubt he'd want to consult the Wish Book for ideas about what to search for on eBay, and thus how to spend the money his parents would send him. In the kitchen, Jen opened a door beneath the sink, shoved the catalog into the trash. She buried it deep.

For the last year Jen and Paul had rented the attic of a large white colonial in New Haven, Massachusetts. The house belonged to a pair of twenty-five-year-old identical twins named Alice and Christine, who'd inherited it from their grandmother. The twins were short and pretty and spunky, with green eyes and crimson hair. The house, with its glass doorknobs and high ceilings and steep staircases and brittle windows that trembled whenever a car drove by, hadn't changed since the twins' grandmother died—nor had it been thoroughly cleaned. Antique sofas, covered in cat hair, were unraveling. Dirty plates, abandoned by the twins, attracted swarms of fruit flies. Dust balls, like miniature tumbleweeds, drifted across the wood floors. The kitchen reeked of sour milk and wet cat food, thanks to the series of bowls the twins had left out for a wild-eyed Persian that brought dead mice into the house and trailed fluorescent bits of kitty litter from its fur.

"You don't have to do that," Christine said. She was eating a health bar in the breakfast nook while Jen scrubbed a pot one of the twins had left on the stove. A scorched lump of angel hair clung to the bottom.

"I don't mind," Jen said. She didn't. Work, she hoped, might prevent her from summoning the head. Only she kept shutting her eyes to see if it was still there. It was. Its nostrils quivered as if preparing to sneeze. In her mind Jen slipped a hand through its neck hole and encountered a warm, suctiony passageway. She wormed around, found its brain: an eggy gelatin pulsing with electricity. The head liked this. It shuddered. Its lips parted, revealing a set of crumbly teeth.

"Last night," Jen said, "I dreamed John the Baptist's head was singing to me."

Christine shoved the last chunk of her breakfast bar into her mouth. "Weird," she said. She ripped a sheet of paper from a pad on the refrigerator. She handed Jen the paper and a miniature pencil. "Write it down."

"Write what down?"

"What you just said."

Jen stared at the paper. In the bottom right-hand corner, a woman held a broom and a mop and a bucket and sponges in her arms. A caption read: Domestically Disabled. Jen squeezed the pen, drew the letters neatly across the top of the page.

Years before, Christine and Alice had taught themselves the basics of handwriting analysis. On several occasions, they'd scrutinized the phone messages Jen had taken, her grocery lists, her rent checks. Every time, it seemed to Jen like they were playing a trick on her; no matter how hard she tried to print the letters correctly, her writing always betrayed a number of personal deficiencies. She suffered from a lack of this, she yearned for more of that.

Christine held the paper at arm's length. "Okay. You wrote the sentence at the topmost part of the page. That actually suggests a high degree of ambition. Good. You also left-aligned everything, which probably represents a desire to be grounded by family or friends. At the same time, the spacing between your letters is saying... give me breathing space. What really stands out, though, is that you have a tendency to slant left."

"What's that mean?"

"It could mean you're depressed. But most likely you're afraid."

"Afraid of what?"

"Don't get defensive," Christine replied. "I just interpret what I see."

That afternoon Jen returned to the room in the White House. Her eyes burned; she'd spent a good deal of the day trying not to shut them. Unless she made a conscious choice to keep them open, her lids had a tendency, every ten to fifteen blinks, to seal themselves shut. When this happened, the head appeared. It shook itself back and forth, slapping itself with its hair. Its lips mouthed the word no over and over. She understood what it meant: she'd promised herself she wouldn't attend the same class twice. But who was the head to tell her what to do? She made the rules. She could revise them.

As students took their seats, Jen hid behind a copy of the school newspaper. She read a student poem about the beauty of ice, scanned an editorial complaining about the price of cafeteria food, as well as an article discussing the work of Ron Peabody, North Atlantic's sole art teacher. The newspaper had reprinted Peabody's most recent work: a painting of a girl with tangled hair tethered to a weird-looking cross—one that, upon closer inspection, Jen realized had been made from three partially engorged phalli. It looked to Jen like a terrible painting; apparently, others had reacted similarly. Ron Peabody's defense? It was supposed to be terrible: it was about sexual abuse.

Eventually, a rumpled, sharp-featured man with graying sideburns entered the room. He shuffled through a briefcase, removed a sheet of paper, and began calling roll. Jen's body pulsed, as though a host of live tiny things was pressing against the inside of her skin. There was only one explanation: she'd gone to the wrong class.

She tapped the shoulder of the boy next to her. The boy had cornrows and a thin beard that ran along his jawline and around his lips—a beard so neat and trim it looked like it might've been drawn with a Magic Marker. "What class is this?" she asked.

"Intro to Humanities," he said.

"Who's that?"

"Professor Wood. You didn't hear about Laycock? She was walking her dog last night and keeled over. Heart attack. Out for the semester. Maybe forever."

"Anyone's name I did not call?" Professor Wood asked. "Okay, then. Let's begin with a prayer."

Jen shut her eyes. The head swung back and forth, a pendulum of hairy meat. Professor Wood asked for a blessing upon the class, the school, and especially Dr. Laycock. The head moved its lips to Wood's words. Jen pinched herself several times on the thigh, hoping her brain would interpret the code: Cut it out.

After the prayer, Wood apologized. He would not be discussing the symbolist movement. Nor, for that matter, would he discuss any branch of the humanities. He would spend his time here discussing what he knew: ecology. All the people in this room were earthbound creatures; thus, they were stewards of the earth and its resources. "How many of you shower every day?" he asked. Hands flew up. "And why," Wood asked, "do you do this?"

The boy with the perfect goatee raised his hand. "We're dirty," he said.

"Really?" Wood said. "Are you slopping hogs? Slaughtering calves? Shoveling manure? At the very least you're probably walking at least five miles to school everyday, right? No? That's what your ancestors were doing a hundred years ago, and they went entire weeks without bathing. But you guys need one every day? Here's a challenge for you: skip that bath two days a week. Use the same towel for a month. Learn to use less!"

Goatee Boy passed Jen a note. Didn't catch yr name, it said. I'm Lorenzo.

Jen thought for a second. Linda, she wrote, taking care to slant every letter right-ward. I'm new. From Canada.

You cute, Lorenzo wrote back.

"You think," Wood said, "that because this world isn't our eternal home we can trash it? Man was given dominion, yes, but dominion means control. And if we don't conserve, folks, we won't be in control. We'll be awash in chaos."

Jen folded the note. She flipped open her notebook. She wrote stewards at the top of the page, drew a question mark after. Stewards slanted right, but the question mark stood up straight. It stood at attention. It looked ready for battle.

After class, Jen asked Lorenzo what he knew about John the Baptist.

"The voice crying in the wilderness," Lorenzo said, smiling. He was typing a message on his phone; every few seconds his lips parted, revealing a luminous wad of gum. "You know. He predicted Jesus and all that. Then baptized him."

"Not that," Jen said. "The stuff about his head."

Lorenzo flipped his phone shut. "You mean the ho who asked for it on a platter? Who knows why those people did what they did. Last week? In Faith of our Fathers? We read this story from Judges where this old dude gives away a concubine, along with his virgin daughter, to a gang of men to rape all night. Then, in the morning, the old dude takes the concubine and chops her into twelve pieces."

"That's a true story?"

Lorenzo wrapped an arm around Jen's shoulder. His fingers, which grazed her neck, were soft and slightly sticky. "Of course it's true," he said. "It's Scripture."

"But what does it mean? A king offers you half his kingdom, and you ask for a decapitated head?"

"You're not a big Bible person, are you?"

"What makes you say that?"

"You don't give off that vibe. Which is fine. But you should come to that class. You'd get a kick out of Bowers. He's a trip."

At the religion department—a tall, yellow Victorian flanked by tall maples—Jen followed Lorenzo through the front door and into a room that resembled a chapel. He sat down on the back pew beside an Asian girl wearing a baggy sweatshirt and spandex pants. She was sucking a purple lollipop.

"You know Joanne?" Lorenzo asked.

"Um," Jen said.

"Linda's from Canada," Lorenzo explained.

"Didn't you used to be in Approaches to Literature?" Joanne asked.

"I dropped that," Jen said.

"I wish I'd dropped it," Joanne replied. "But today, oh my gosh, Lorenzo. Do you know Greg?"

"Red-cheeked boy with the fro?"

Joanne nodded. She popped her sucker in and out of her mouth. "We were supposed to look up an old song, as old as we could possibly find, and bring the lyrics in. When it's his turn, he starts reading some song he found from the thirteenth century or whatever. But the lyrics are all about this dude dripping candle wax on this woman's… you know."

"Hoo-ha?" Lorenzo said.

"Only, he didn't say 'hoo-ha.' He said the C word. But the way he said it, it was like he didn't even know what it meant!"

"Get out," Lorenzo said.

"I swear."

"You ever tried it?" Jen asked.

"Excuse me?" Joanne replied.

"Have you had anyone drip candle wax onto your C-word?"

Joanne frowned. "Um, no?"

"And you?" Lorenzo asked, aiming his finger at Jen.

"I'm still waiting for the right person."

Lorenzo chuckled.

"Your friend's funny," Joanne said. She wasn't smiling. "Is everybody this funny in Canada?"

Jen didn't have time to answer. Doug Bowers, the bemused-looking blond man who taught Faith of Our Fathers, had begun a recap of last week's lecture on the Millerite movement: using the books of Ezekiel and Daniel, the Millerites had created a system by which they predicted the Second Coming of Christ. Followers donned ascension robes, sold their worldly possessions, and waited in graveyards for a dark little cloud to bloom angels. October 22, 1844, came and went. Nothing happened. The Millerites were disappointed. Greatly.

"It's hard for me to believe," said a bearded man in the front pew, "that nobody pointed out Matthew 25:13 to these folks."

"Ah!" Bowers said. "Don't be so quick to judge! A revolution in faith is a complicated event. Most of the time, there are more than a few kinks to work out."

A chubby, sour-faced girl raised her hand. "Should somebody explain Matthew 25? Not everyone's memorized the Bible."

"Watch therefore," the bearded man said, "for ye know not neither the day nor the hour wherein the Son of man cometh."

"Thanks," the girl said, smirking.

"Remember," Bowers said, "it's easy to identify the flaws of our ancestors. A hundred years from now, our own children will probably look back at us and say 'What morons!' Our main concern, the one that should keep us up at night, is this: are we searching Scripture as closely as the Millerites? Are we seeking our own personal revelations?"

After class, Lorenzo slipped Jen a strip of paper with his number; he had to run. He had basketball practice from two to four. Jen stuffed the paper into her pocket and waited for Bowers. She had a question for him: could modern-day people have visions?

"I'm sure they can," Bowers said. "The question is, what kind?"

"That's what I wanted to find out. See, I have this friend. She keeps having the same dream, even when she's awake."

"Sounds like this friend of yours needs to search her heart. As well as Scripture."

"But what if what she's seeing is straight from the Bible?"

Bowers shook his head. "You have to be so careful with visions. There's always the chance that it's originating in some other, darker place. The truth is, no one on this planet knows the Bible like the devil."

"The devil?"

"I'm not talking about a cartoon guy with horns and a pitchfork. I'm talking about a beautiful fallen angel. The one-time leader of the heavenly choir. A being with the power to seduce the hearts and minds of the Very Elect. A being who rejoices every time a human refuses to believe in him. Because think about it: you can't resist an influence if you don't even believe it exists."

Back at the twins' house, Paul and Alice and Christine were at the dining room table, playing a board game Paul had recently won in an eBay auction. The game involved rolling a pair of dice, turning a clock, and sticking your finger into the mouth of a plastic vampire. The point was to hope the vampire didn't wake up. If he did, he'd bite your finger. His felt-tipped fangs would leave two dots behind, thus branding you a loser.

"Hey," Paul said. "You ever find that Wish Book?"

"No," Jen replied. She brushed a few specks of dandruff from his shoulder.

"I have got to find that thing."

"Wanna play the next round?" Christine asked.

"I'm good," Jen replied.

"So," Alice said, "how was school?"

"You mean college," Paul said.

"Good," Jen said. "I learned about the Millerite movement."

Paul frowned. "I thought you were taking science classes."

Jen shrugged. "We had a guest speaker."

Alice, a self-proclaimed history buff, cleared her throat dramatically. "Paul?" she said. "I'm going to have to take issue with that assumption. The Millerite movement wasn't totally unscientific. In fact, if I'm not mistaken, I remember a number of Millerites becoming quite active in various health movements. Which makes sense. There's nothing more scientific than learning how to take care of your body, especially when preparing oneself for translation." Alice stuck her finger into the vampire's mouth. She waited. The clock ticked. Nothing happened.

"Translation?" Jen asked.

"The journey from earth to heaven. The Millerites believed you had to exclude from your diet any foods that aroused the animal passions."

"Sexual desires," Paul explained.

"Exactly," Alice said.

"Nobody said anything about animal passions," Jen said.

"That's the thing about schools like that," Christine added. She blew on the dice in her hand, then released them. "There's a lot about stuff they never tell you."

Jen made an announcement: she was exhausted. "Good night," said the twins. "Good night," said Paul. Jen climbed the stairs to the second floor, then a final flight to the attic. She held a cordless phone and a strip of paper with a string of numbers and the name LORENZO RAMON ALFARO. She sat on the futon. She rubbed her eyes. Surprise, surprise: the head appeared. It was not happy. It was weeping. But it didn't have tears to cry, only blood. Was it a test? Jen wondered. She decided that it was. The head wanted to know if she felt for it.

"You're sad," Jen whispered.

I yearn for what I have not.

"Your body?"

The head tried to answer, but couldn't. It was overcome by its weeping. Jen imagined cradling it in her arms. Every time, it slipped from her grasp.

Please, the head said. Its bottom lip quivered. Think of Linda. Of Lorenzo.

Jen opened her eyes. How could a head so sad be all that bad? The answer, she guessed, was in the letters of Lorenzo's number, which she punched into the phone. She waited.

"It's Linda," she said, when he picked up.

"What's up?"

Good question, Jen thought. What would Linda say? Linda: a woman with a free ride, a woman with a vision. A woman without fear, who knew what she wanted and believed she would get it. "You like to party?" Jen asked.

"Depends what you mean by 'party.'"

"Party. P. A. R. T. Y. Party."

"If you mean party, drink, then nah. I ain't down with that. Gotta keep my temple clean."

"I'm thinking maybe something with candlelight. Some hot wax."

Lorenzo laughed. "You're crazy. I gotta study!"

A nasal laugh echoed in the background. "Is that Joanne?"

"Yeah."

"Aha."

"Nah, it ain't like that. She's in Abnormal Psych with me. We got a huge-ass test tomorrow."

"What's more important? Studying for a test or unlocking an ancient mystery?"

"You still tripping about John the Baptist?"

"I'm not tripping. Just seeking new truths."

"You should chill. Let those truths come to you."

"Maybe you should teach me."

"Maybe I will. I'll play you some music. Tomorrow, you and me. I'll write you a song."

"A song about the head of John the Baptist?"

"Yes. Exactly. Promise. Cross my heart. Hope to die."

"Don't disappoint me."

"This is Lorenzo you talking to."

"Lorenzo," she said. "Lorenzo, Lorenzo, let down your hair." She hung up the phone. Her body was alive with palpitations. But actually she felt great. When the head appeared in her mind, she addressed it. What did it think? Should she follow through? The head wasn't talking. It appeared to be sleeping. "I'll call the whole thing off now if you tell me," she whispered. The head kept its lips zipped. Maybe the head knew she was bluffing. The head, she figured, could see right through her.

"It doesn't make sense," Paul said. "Things don't just disappear."

"You're in love with things," Jen said. For the last ten minutes, they'd been lying on the futon, trying to retrace where the Wish Book had gone. "I mean, like, physical things. You love them."

"I'm a materialist," Paul explained. "I make no apologies for that."

"It wasn't a criticism," Jen said. "Just a fact."

"Some might see it as a flaw."

"Only if it interferes with your life."

"It sort of is my life."

"That's one way we're different from each other. I can't think of anything I own that I wouldn't mind giving up."

"I like to hold on to things," Paul said. He slipped his hand inside her shirt. "You, for instance."

"Please," Jen said.

He mashed himself against her backside. "Wanna do something?"

Do something. It meant did she want him to touch her while he touched himself? Which was what he liked. He liked other things—he liked the normal things, and the normal ways—but this was what he preferred.

"I don't know," she said. "I haven't showered in a while."

"A while?"

"Two days. No. Three."

"Why?"

"Conserving water is important."

"But so is personal hygiene."

"We're stewards, you know."

"Stewards?"

"Of the earth."

"You're being weird."

"What's so weird about having a conscience?"

"If you're not interested," he said, "all you have to do is say so."

"I'm not interested."

"Fine," he said. He flipped over. The futon shook.

"Good night," Jen said. He didn't answer. She didn't close her eyes. She kept them peeled. The stars faded. The head congealed.

You refused him love, it said.

He's had plenty of love, Jen thought.

Can such things be measured?

Okay, Jen thought, so maybe you couldn't measure love. But sex? Sex you definitely measure. And in that department Paul had her beat. She knew; he'd told her the stories. Stories she hadn't wanted to hear: ropes, honey, milk, blood, blindfolds. The psycho exes, the ones who'd do anything, then make him regret it.

But he's yours now, the head said. Your first. Your last.

The head had a point. This troubled her. She did not want to be troubled. She wanted the head to shut up. But really: how? The answer, she discovered, was frightening: you harnessed the power of the unthinkable. Could she think the unthinkable? Could she imagine, for instance, removing all her clothes? Could she imagine spreading her legs? Could she imagine sitting on the head—on its upturned face—and riding it until it suffocated? She could not. She didn't want to take it that far. She didn't want to imagine herself rocking back and forth on the face of a head, especially a holy one. No rocking, she told herself as she began to move. No rocking.

Paul was shouting her name.

"What?"

"You were laughing."

She'd been dreaming. In the dream, she'd been standing on George Hill, a mound of treeless earth on the edge of North Atlantic College that kids used in winter for sledding. She'd gone there to get rid of the head. She'd jammed two fingers into its eye sockets, hooked her thumb under its top row of teeth, then hurled it down the hill like a bowling ball. She punted it into the sky. She slung it. She chucked it. Every time, the head rolled back. Every time, she was mad, but then the head would stick out its tongue or make kissy faces and she would laugh.

"I had a dream," she said. "A nightmare."

"Oh boy," Paul replied.

"You never want to hear my dreams."

"I never want to hear anybody's."

Paul was wearing a pink oxford shirt and pink polyster pants. His hair was pink. He had a pair of pink lensless glasses and pink deely-bobbers on his head.

"Check this out," he said. He slapped a sticker over his heart. It said: HELLO my name is FLOYD. "Get it?"

"But it's not even Halloween," Jen said.

"The store's having a contest," Paul said. "You have to wear your costume for a week in-store to be eligible to win. And guess who's gonna come home with a fifty-dollar gift certificate?" He kissed her forehead. His stubble left a burn.

Jen had almost forgotten: she had a date. Not a real date. A fake date. The date, after all, was not rightly hers: Linda had done all the work. Linda and Lorenzo. It had a certain ring, didn't it? Linda and Lorenzo had planned to meet in the Conservatory, a gargantuan building that had once been a sanitarium, and which was now home to the North Atlantic Department of Music. "The Conservatory?" Linda had asked. "For real? Will Colonel Mustard be there? Should I bring a candlestick?" Lorenzo didn't get the joke. "You're Clue-less!" Linda had exclaimed. He didn't get that one either. Which was okay. The important thing, Jen realized, was to keep Linda laughing. Linda was decidedly upbeat. Linda was the kind of person who had the power, no matter what the circumstance, to stay positive.

"You know about the tunnels, right?" Lorenzo said. They'd met in the lobby, peeked in on an a cappella group holding their mouths as they sang, Yo-ho, yo-ho, yo-ho-whoa! Now, they climbed a creaking staircase blanketed with dingy red carpet.

"What tunnels?" Linda couldn't take her eyes off Lorenzo's hair. He had let it out, as she requested. It was now a glistening poof ball on the top of his head.

"I've personally never seen them," Lorenzo said. "Just heard they were there."

"Like the underground railroad," Linda said.

"Maybe."

"Did your ancestors ever use such transportation?"

Lorenzo laughed. "I wish," he said, opening a door in a dim hallway. "My ancestors came from Brazil."

The door opened into a tiny room—one barely big enough to hold a piano. It smelled of dust and rotting wood. Sunlight poured through a window smeared with fingerprints, filling the room with haze. Lorenzo sat on the bench, his fingers splayed across the keys. "This one," he said, "is called 'The Voice Crying in the Wilderness.'"

Lorenzo couldn't read a note. He made everything up as he went. His fingers, Jen noticed, were long and elegant, his nails so polished they looked fake. He frowned meaningfully while he played, tilting his head this way and that. Every once in a while, he let out a moan. Unfortunately, the song failed to live up to its title. It sounded like something from Mister Rogers' Neighborhood.

"How do you know what to play?" Jen asked.

"It just comes to me."

"So you hear it first?"

"Sometimes."

"Do you ever hear anything you don't want to play?"

"Like what?" Lorenzo said. He lifted his hands off the keys. The chord he'd just played dissolved.

"Sometimes, I hear things. Like a voice. A higher power."

"You should listen to it."

"But I'm not even sure I believe in a higher power."

"We all have our doubts," Lorenzo said. He ran a finger along her jawline. She tensed. Her back felt like it was breaking out into hives.

"How do you get over that?" she asked.

"You just take a look around. You acknowledge that God's in everything. Everything that's alive, everything that is, is from God. Think about it. If you were to have a child, that child would have your blood, your genetic code, right? Well, every piece of material around you was made by God, which means it's been imprinted with His code. That's what's so fly about science. It's just you checking everything out and what's being revealed is God's code. You make connections, you start understanding, but you never get full. The more you eat, the hungrier you get."

"Mm," Jen said.

"Like right now, looking at you, I'm seeing God's code all over the place."

Lorenzo sucked on her bottom lip, pulling it into his mouth. Jen closed her eyes. The head was bobbing in a river of blood. It was trying to drink from this river, but every time it tipped over and reached out its tongue, the head flipped back over onto its back. Jen opened her eyes. Lorenzo's eyes bulged beneath their lids. They jerked back and forth, like they wanted out of their sockets.

Things were moving fast. What would Linda think about Lorenzo unbuttoning her jeans? Was Linda that easy? She was. Definitely. Then why was she whispering no? Was Linda one of those types? Would she whisper no with her mouth but say yes with her body? Could Linda welcome the hands of Lorenzo even though they were freezing? Did she have a choice? His hands, which had recently been at work inside Linda's pants, were now at work upon their own. Did Lorenzo have protection? Linda wanted to know. "Protection from what?" Lorenzo asked. "From babies," Linda said. "From diseases. From diseased babies." Lorenzo assured her it was all good; he was clean. "Okay, but," Linda said. "Wait a second," she said, though it was clear there would be no waiting involved. Not today. Don't you think. Shouldn't we. I don't know if. Hey. Wait. Wait. And then came the decision of Linda's that surprised Jen the most: she did not move. She stayed perfectly still.

Lorenzo wanted to know if Linda was okay. Of course she was! She was just waiting a sec to put on her pants. After being so full, that part of her needed to breathe. What about him? Was he okay? Yeah. Definitely. But you know what? He needed to jet. "I need to jet," he'd said. "Need" meaning "want." "Jet" meaning get quickly to basketball practice. He was already late. "Late" meaning he wished he was already there. He would call. Everything cool? She nodded.

But everything was not cool. As Jen pedaled the twins' bike toward campus, her crotch burned. The stinging was so bad that she stopped at the old cemetery across from the main campus. The gravestones were thin, dark grey slabs, slanting in different directions. She deemed the left-slanters weak, the right-slanters strong. The bodies buried here had names like Silas and Elias and James. Alive once, in another century.

It was a beautiful day for a funeral. The sun was splashing all over the green leaves; a swarm of insects danced overhead: tiny dots of light. They swirled around each other, separating and dispersing, then collecting themselves again in a cascading swarm. Winds came and bore them upward, flinging them across the cemetery. They floated on the air like yellow bits of light materialized. Jen moved toward them. She wished to be carried away. Something flew into her nose.

The committee room in the White House was dark and full of students. A man who was not Dr. Laycock or Professor Wood stood at the front of the class. He resembled a fat, balding Sean Connery. Jen had seen him before, driving a red Miata. Then she remembered: Anthony Muntz. Ph.D., Old Dominion.

Jen made her way to the front of the table. The head of the class, she thought. She could see Muntz up close. His wide nostrils were dark passageways heading into his face. Muntz pointed a remote at a slide projector he'd crammed into the corner of the room. A phantasmagoric worm appeared on the screen, its gaping mouth bearing what looked like two fangs.

"Hookworm!" Muntz exclaimed. "Didn't know you had these little suckers inside you, did you? I'm kidding. Sort of.

Some of you do and some of you don't. Anybody in here like meat? Congratulations! You just upped your chances of getting a pinworm. Familiar with the pinworm? Lives in your rectum. Comes out at night, lays eggs in your anus. Anybody got an itchy behind? No? Means nothing. Parasites don't just live in your bowels, people. These little guys pop up all over. Heart, head, lungs. Even your eyes."

Jen mashed hers shut. Oblongs of light swarmed against the darkness. The head rolled. It bore its crumbly teeth. It looked like it might be in agony.

"You guys like magic?" Muntz asked. The audience mumbled. Somebody cackled. "Of course you do. Everybody likes magic. I'm gonna do a little magic. But I need a volunteer."

Jen raised her hand.

"Okay Miss Enthusiasm," he said. "Come on up."

She went.

Muntz squeezed her arm with one hand and with another, swiped a Q-tip across her forehead. Then he wiped the Q-tip onto a slide, slid it under the microscope projector. Muntz focused the microscope. Something came into view. It looked like a short, fat eel, with little suckers up front for legs. It had the face of a catfish.

"Aha!" Muntz said. "Beautiful. Wonderful. Sometimes it takes a couple swabs. But you, my dear, you're a veritable parasite production company. Just kidding. Probably just got lucky. Everybody's got 'em! Anybody know what we're looking at here? No? Demodex folliculorum! Don't let the name scare you. Little bugger's harmless, long as it doesn't multiply too much. Last thing you want's papulopustular rosacea. But you, my dear, you don't have to worry about that. Just keep your head clean."

The bell rang. Jen stared at the screen for a minute, then followed the others outside. The sun was bright. It seemed like it should be lower than it was. Demodex folliculorum, she thought.

An incantation. A summons.

At the twins' house, Jen made the executive decision: time to clean. She dusted. She organized. She mopped. She got on her hands and knees, ground the nozzle of the Wet Vac into Oriental rugs to suck up cat hair. Hours later, everything still looked filthy. It would, she realized, take weeks to right what had gone wrong here; it was stupid to have started. In the downstairs bathroom, she found a dead leaf. She looked at it hard. It wasn't a dead leaf. It was a dead mouse head. It was looking right at her. She waited for it to speak. It didn't.

Someone was pounding on the front door. She opened it to find Lorenzo, drenched in sweat. His jersey, which said NAC Flames, was soaked. He'd run the whole way here. He was hiding something behind his back.

"I wanted to make sure you were cool," he said.

"How did you know where I live?"

"You think I don't know where my girl lives?"

"Your girl?"

"I brought you something." He held out a single red rose.

Jen shook her head. "I'm engaged," she said. "To be married."

Lorenzo's tongue wormed around, making one of his cheeks bulge outward. He raised his eyebrows. "Damn," he said. "Why didn't you say nothing?"

"I tried," Jen said. "You weren't listening."

"Wait," he said. "This mean you ain't coming to my game tonight?"

Jen slammed the door. She waited for him to knock again. He didn't.

Down in the twins' cellar, Jen helped herself to the oldest bottle of Bordeaux she could find. She tried to open the bottle with a wine key, but broke the cork. She shoved the rest of the cork into the bottle with a chopstick. She poured half the bottle into a Big Gulp cup. Shards of cork bobbed on the surface like the remnants of a shipwreck. Upstairs she searched the twins' bookcases for a Bible, found one, turned to the index, looked up John the Baptist. The Gospel of Matthew had this to say: Among those born of women, there has not risen anyone greater than John the Baptist; yet he who is least in the kingdom of heaven is greater than he. In the fourteenth chapter, she found the story of the beheading. Salome's mother had asked for the head of John the Baptist; John the Baptist had called her an adulteress. Jen wasn't sure, but it seemed like Salome's mother had slept with another man. Apparently, nobody knew this but God, who told John the Baptist.

Dr. Laycock hadn't mentioned a mother. Dr. Laycock had said nothing about a mother. Jen felt like she should be mad, but then she thought of Laycock, wasting away. Who would teach her class from now on? Who would walk her dog? A sixty-year-old woman. No children. No husband. Probably never been laid. But maybe she didn't need sex. Instead of sex, she planted ideas into the heads of her students, and hoped they'd grow wild.

"You cleaned," Paul said, when he came home. He tore open a strawberry fruit roll up. He dangled it above his face. It looked like skin. Like raw, sticky meat. He lowered it into his mouth and chomped.

"You can't really clean this place," she said. "There's like, a gazillion centuries of filth on everything. ou try to clean and it spreads out. It moves."

"Have you been drinking?"

"Nooo," Jen said, wrapping her arms around his torso. "Not much. Hardly any."

"You reek."

"Did you know that people of yore hardly ever bathed?"

"You are wasted. Which might explain the fact that you don't seem to remember what day it is."

"I do remember," Jen said. "It's the day of Lorenzo's game."

"Who's Lorenzo?"

"Lorenzo," Jen said. "The basketball player. My lover. Did you know I'd taken a lover?"

"I'm going downstairs," Paul said. "Call me when you've sobered up."

How did Jen get to the gym? She thought she'd walked but she couldn't remember the journey. She knew only that the gym was hot and cramped and packed with students. There were a few feet between the end of the court and the beginning of the concrete wall. The Flames were beating Southern Vermont by twenty-five. Every time Lorenzo got the ball, he scored. He dribbled between his legs, head faked right, went left, spun, leaped into the air, double-pumped, and shot. It made her head hurt to watch. She could barely keep up. Clearly, he was the star.

In the bleachers—on a balcony at the north end of the gym—the students were going crazy.

Afterwards, Jen watched Lorenzo stand in line to slap the palms of the opposing team. Streaks of light swam over his sweaty skin. Joanne, wearing a gymnastics uniform, came running out of the crowd. She jumped onto him. He wrapped his arms around her. Apparently, she didn't mind the sweat. She embraced him with her legs. He kissed her on the mouth.

"Lorenzo," Jen yelled. She thought she might flip him off. He never looked up.

"Hey," a voice said. It was the sour-faced girl from Faith of Our Fathers. She was wearing a Marilyn Manson tank-top and green eyeliner. Her arms, the size of Jen's thighs, were bare and smeared with red splotches. One of them, Jen noticed, looked like a face. A face with a beard and no body.

"My friends and I have a bet," she said. "They don't think you go here, but I told them you're in my class."

"Oh."

"Can you do me a favor and just tell them you go here?"

Jen glanced over the sour-faced girl's shoulder, to the top of the bleachers. Two short black girls—they looked barely thirteen—turned away and giggled.

"I don't go here," Jen said. "Not anymore."

Paul sat at the head of the dining room table, surrounded by a mound of Super Friends wrapping paper. His hair was still pink, but he'd changed into his Captain America shirt—the one he'd bought at Target, the one that'd been faded to look old.

His birthday? Was that possible? Had she missed it again? It came every year on the same day and every year she found a way to forget. This time she'd also missed the gift-opening. The table was crowded with mint-condition toys: monster puppets, squishy, baseball-sized balls with gruesome faces. Alice tossed a glob of slime—green and lustrous and wobbly—between her hands; Christine snap a monstrous skull onto a plastic skeleton.

"I had a revelation," Paul said. "I'm twenty-nine years old. Today is the first day of the last year of my youth. What better way to celebrate than busting open the mint condition boxes of yesteryear?"

"Our children's inheritance," Jen said.

"Who better to spend it on than ourselves?"

Christine handed Paul the miniature skeleton, which she'd plastered with clay. Paul ripped open a packet of Powdered Monster Flesh Remover. They dropped the monster into the plastic vat. The flesh sizzled. The water began to boil. For a second Jen thought it might come alive. The flesh bubbled away. The water turned green. The twins cheered.

"You want a sundae?" Alice asked. Jen wanted a sundae. She did. But she couldn't bring herself to say so. Sundaes were for good girls and boys. Every good boy deserves fudge. Where had she learned that? She didn't know. It made perfect sense.

"In a minute," she said. "I'm going upstairs to change."

In the attic Jen slid out of her clothes. Naked, she walked across the hall and into the shower, where she twisted the cap off one of the twins' bottles of shampoo. She dumped out a handful, lathered her arms, her legs, her face. Some got in her eyes, mashed them shut. There, in the stinging darkness, the head of John the Baptist hovered. There was nothing scary about it, Jen realized. Nothing sexy. It simply was.

The time has come, the head said. Jen knew what to do. She didn't know how she knew but she did. She saw herself reaching out through the dark to take hold of the head. It prickled with heat. She slid it over her head like a hood—like a mask. It was tight. The inside was slick and sticky and hot. It felt as if fireworks were going off on her face. She understood. The head was fusing itself to her flesh. She opened her eyes. She felt it. It was there. It was on. She couldn't breathe. She tried to speak. She wheezed.

She wrapped herself in a towel and descended the stairs. She gripped the rail. Balancing the new weight was difficult. In the den Paul and the twins were sitting on the couch. Paul balanced a quart of ice cream in his lap. They all had spoons, but they'd stopped using them. They were staring at the TV. She could tell by their faces that something terrible was about to happen. She stood in the doorway. She wasn't in a rush. She would wait all night. She had time. She didn't know what she would say, but she trusted the head to make the right decisions. It knew what they needed to hear. It had known all along what to say. All it had needed, all this time, was a body, to which it could harness itself. She was the one.

"Behold," she said when they finally looked her direction. "My kingdom is at hand."

BODIES

My first night on Pleasure Island, I whiskeyed myself up on the deck of a condo and watched waves pound the beach where the bodies of Confederate and Federal troops had been blown to smithereens. I'd promised Copeland—my former brother-in-law, the man whose condo I'd commandeered—that under no conditions would I drink. It was a stupid thing to say, but I'd said it early in the morning, which meant it didn't count. Most mornings, I'm aswarm with promises. No more this, no more that. Of course, the changed-man bit lasts about half a day. I blame the sun. Post zenith, it tends to slope downward. This downslope takes everything it touches and makes it boozeworthy. As my daddy used to say: "Drink, drink, and drink some more, for tomorrow we die." But tomorrow, more often than not, we do not die. Tomorrow we wake with blood in our shorts and a toothache of the heart, to make promises that seem keepable until the downslope awakens our indefatigable whims.

My bottle was empty. I flipped it into the dunes, where it shushed in the grass. I felt grandiose, famished. I would've spooned the contents of a mayonnaise jar into my face if there'd been any, but Copeland stocked only salt, pepper, sugar, and chamomile tea. So I shuffled three blocks to a shack reeking of grease, ordered a cheese sandwich and a Wild Turkey, neat.

That night, this bar's Magnavox blazed with some self-congratulatory bullshit about sexual predators. A host with a face based loosely on the face of a human had made himself available over the internet. There he'd claimed to be a thirteen-year-old girl who wanted to party; now he was hosting a sting operation. Guys streamed into a McMansion and the

Host confronted them, and they either prayed for mercy or
claimed they'd brought condoms and beer for educational
purposes. Afterward, the cops, wearing bulletproof vests,
threw them to the ground, read them their rights. I told the
bartender the only way I'd continue to watch this trash was
if the Host snipped off their cocks and crammed them down
their throats. "Easy," said my neighbor, some young buck with
clippered hair and tatted arms, the usual bozo who thinks
because he's lifted some weights he can police whatever
vicinity he finds himself in.

I knew from experience that guys like him were all
mouth and flabby muscle. Problem was they hadn't spent
much time in the ring; their jaws were champagne-flute glass.
So what if you were an old sack of jellied gristle? If you'd survived a few bouts and owned a switchblade you'd been
carrying since eighty-two, you had a better-than-average
chance.

"Once upon a time," I said, "a bastard hacked my daughter
to pieces."

"Sorry to hear that," the young buck replied.

"That's not the story," I said. "The story is that ten years
later I watched a state employee shove a needle chock-full of
poison into that bastard's arm. I watched him die. And you
know what? I liked it. In fact, when they flipped the switch
and his body started flopping, I cheered. But it turned out
cheering wasn't the thing to do. My rejoicing carved out a
nasty hollow. It taught me something. Take no pleasure in
the harm you mean to have done."

"Sir," the young buck said. "Get out of my face."

I flipped out the blade. The guy raised his hands.

"That'll do," the bartender said. He was all skin and
bones, with a face that suggested he might've tasted a rest-

room floor. And at the end of his tanned, hairless arm, there was a polished .38.

I tossed a ten on the bar, said, "Keep the change."

Like a true hot-shot, I woke up in the sand, among broken seashells and cigarette butts and ice cream wrappers and those plastic discs you snap on the tops of soda cups. I dragged myself into a sitting position, smacked ants from my legs, and stared at the churning sea. It occurred to me that Primordial Man might've watched a similar sunrise bleed across this same froth. He had not, however, smelled dough-nuts, and that was one of a few things I could think of that separated his world from mine.

On the boardwalk, House of Doughnuts had raised its garage door and was ready to serve. The woman manning the counter was a tall, haggard granny wearing a knee brace, al-ready sweating. On wobbly legs tattooed with Looney Tunes, she retrieved a sack of fried dough for the last guy who needed one, a fatso wearing a red Redskins sweatshirt with the sleeves ripped off, who nodded and smiled at me, making me feel shitty for having silently cursed his bovine physique.

"Need help?" Granny asked.

"I'm thinking," I said. The menu couldn't have been sim-pler. To eat: doughnuts, glazed. To drink: milk and coffee, small or large. They didn't take American Express—only cash. I was about to ask for a sample, when a girl trotted in, maybe twelve, no more than thirteen. Blond braids. Brown, calflike legs, unshaven, adorned with thousands of golden hairs. To say she was a duplicate of my daughter would be saying it wrong. She was my daughter. Which meant she'd ei-ther come back from the dead, or I was really bad off.

The girl ordered a dozen doughnuts. Looney Tunes Legs

fetched them in no time. So. Not a ghost. I was bad off. Worse than I'd thought. She unwadded a few bills for the granny. I followed her out. I tried to stay at a safe distance, or maybe I didn't, because I caught up to her, tapped her shoulder. She whirled around; a braid tip brushed my outstretched hand. A harrowing sight I made for sure, a scorched lump, aglitter with sand. But she didn't scream. Squinting, she waited for me to explain.

"I'm sorry," I said. "For a minute I thought, maybe."

"What?"

I knelt. The earth was tilting. The Lord, I figured, trying to knock me down. "I thought," I wheezed, "you were some-body."

"You okay?" She pulled a phone from her hoodie pocket. "I can call 911."

I shook my head. "It's just the downslope."

She frowned. "Forget it. I'm old," I explained.

"Angela," a voice said. A man stood at the other end of the alley.

"You don't look that old," she said.

"Angela Simmons!" the voice said again.

"I gotta go," she whispered. She jogged toward the voice, which belonged to a dude laden with muscle, wearing a base-ball hat, sunglasses, and Croakies. He yanked her by the arm, a gesture she'd hold on to, to fuel some misplaced father-hate. She couldn't understand how he needed to feel like he was in charge. Like he had the power to save her. It was a feeling no man could spoil. Unless one came along and did.

I pledged to stay away from the boardwalk. Half an hour later I still hadn't left. Slumped in the bucket seat of a race-car game, watching the monitor advertise itself, I was going nowhere, fast. I had yet to make my mark. Across the room, a toddler sporting fake fangs rode a mechanical, sombreroed donkey. The girl, the one from before, stood beside him. She looked bored. She wiggled a foot from one of her sandals, used it to scratch the back of her other leg. She caught me watching and raised her hand. I didn't wave back. She approached.

"Are you feeling better?" she asked. This touched me. It angered me.

"You shouldn't talk to people like me," I said.

She blinked her blue eyes. Her tongue poked the inside of her cheek. My chest prickled, as though a fuse had been lit there. "What kind of person are you?"

"The kind to avoid."

"Do you know Jesus Christ?" she asked. She had a plastic spider ring on one of her fingers. Her lips gleamed with gloss.

"I've heard the name."

"Well, you should know that He's real and He loves you." She opened a coin purse smothered with stickers of wild safari animals, retrieved two quarters and dropped them into my slot.

On the screen, numbers counted down: 3, 2, 1. A green light lit up, and all the cars but mine took off. I stomped the gas. "It might seem okay to think that now," I said, "but what if the unthinkable had a mind to descend?" She didn't answer. I glanced behind me. She was gone. The little mechanical pony was still going, riderless. My car—a yellow Lamborghini—burst into flames.

At House of Doughnuts, a new waitress manned the helm. Buxom was the word for her, big in all the places where you want big to be, except for the eyes, which were about three sizes too large, and a chin that seemed embarrassed by its weakness. The eyes I could deal with as long as I didn't have to look into them. Her flesh was a luxurious brown, peppered with melanomas. Brown hair waterfalled to her ass and shivered when she walked. I waited on a stool. She took care of the others, approached me.

"Where'd Looney Tunes go?" I asked.

"Looney Tunes?" she repeated, frowning and grinning.

"Tall Granny? Had Bugs and Taz waltzing across her calves."

"Mom?"

"Really?"

"That's what we call her. I'm filling in. What can I get you?"

"One quart of whiskey."

"How about a large milk?"

I gazed, unabashedly, at her bosom. "I haven't got a dime," I said.

She winked. "How about we say this one's on me."

Gloria had an apartment two blocks from the beach. She'd refused to retire to my condo because it belonged to a man she didn't know, who rented to people she didn't know, particles of whom had likely been shed throughout, and she didn't much care to breathe these particles, or converge with possible secretions. She'd seen a 20/20 where they hired a forensics team to dig around in a hotel room post maid service. The team had discovered unspeakable discharge, and now it was difficult—impossible, even—for Gloria to inhabit private places where other people had lived.

The funny thing being this: she was a bird lady. I should've guessed by her dangly turquoise earrings that she shared an apartment with such plumage-shedding, shit-producing creatures. The fecundity! I took a whiff before my eyes adjusted to the dark, and despite the tweets, thought pachyderm. The day before, hurricane season had officially begun, so Gloria whipped up some Category Fives—glorified Long Island Iced Teas. Gloria reheated a pot of jambalaya; Michael, the African Grey parrot, perched on my shoulder and nibbled my ear. I was smitten. "Okay," Gloria said, "tell me your story," so I did, touching on my time at a boy's school, how I'd pursued acting, made it as far as a toothpaste commercial, tried my hand as a stuntman, broken both my legs, met my ex-wife at a rodeo, tried real estate, made a fortune, gone bankrupt. In short, I told her nearly everything. As a rule, I won't bring up my daughter with people who don't already know, unless I feel like wasting half a day circumnavigating their sympathies. Instead, I told her what seemed as true as anything else: that my daughter was here on Pleasure Island, that it was a complicated story I might share someday, the most important part being that she'd been sent to live with another family, who'd insisted I never contact her again. Gloria pretended to believe me, asked about my emotional well-being; I assured her it was tolerable. We ate. We drank. We nuzzled. I was pleased to find Gloria's massive legs were as muscular as they looked. I buried my face in her breast, which ponged of coconut. With her legs, she embraced me. I pumped like a drunken teenager; she acted like it was just the thing. Maybe it was. When the blubbering commenced, she didn't inquire. She lapped at my tears, begged me not to stop.

Big surprise: swinging a metal detector feels too much like work, only less fruitful, especially if the battery's dead. I'd found one in a closet at Copeland's, figured it'd transform my pathetic beach amble into something purposeful.

Also I'd filled the pouches of my shorts with airplane bottles of slightly impressive whiskey, charged to a credit card that was about forty dollars from maxed. I clinked as I walked. Waves ate the beach. In fifty years, I predicted, all this would be gone. Then I revised that figure to include the phrase or less.

The girl and her people lounged near the boardwalk, not too far from what appeared to be a family reunion of black folk, some of whom were playing volleyball without a net while the less physically inclined—the swollen and possibly handicapped, wearing massive T-shirts—wallowed in the surf. The girl lay on a towel, next to the smaller boy who'd dug himself an impressive hole. Her parents, youngish and athletic, sat in the shade, wearing sunglasses with silver lenses. Their clothes rippled in the wind. Fifteen feet away, I swung my detector over a mound of incandescent seaweed, reading their lips. I didn't catch much, except for when the father yelled at the kids, reminding them that if they wanted to see Bodyworks they had twenty minutes of beach time. I'd seen a flyer about this thing. People had died, science had claimed their bodies, stripped them of their flesh, snatched out their arteries and organs, shoved it all into the spotlight of a traveling freak show.

I approached the girl's father. "Excuse me," I said. "You believe in reincarnation?"

"Huh?"

"I didn't believe in it, either, until recently."

"Oh," he said, raising his book. "We're not interested, thanks."

"Your daughter," I said. "I had one like her."

"Excuse me?"

"Keep an eye out. Because you never know. The worst

stuff you've never thought is out there. The worst doesn't wait for an invite, either. If I were you, I wouldn't sleep a wink."

"Get the fuck away from my family," he said. He rose from his chair. This guy, unlike the guy from the bar, could've put me in my place. Instead, he unsnapped his phone and punched some numbers. "I'm reporting you," he said.

"Good," I said. Message delivered. Whether he listened or not was up to him. Only he could protect that angel from the hands of an animal who had nothing left to live for, except to hold another man's daughter in his arms.

What I found with the detector turned on: squat.

At Copeland's, I opened a little book that'd been left, by his wife I presumed, for renters to record their flattery. Everyone loved the beach! And the house? The décor was fab! Michael's seafood was awesome. House of Doughnuts rocked! Boy, were they were going to have to lose some weight after this vacation! I read every word of that shitstorm, a testament to the sweet oblivion of the unscathed, and spent the rest of the day trying to generate some compliment to pay Pleasure Island. I came up with one thing only, though my hand wouldn't write it: I want you to sleep in my arms.

The next day, Gloria asked if I wanted to go see the bodies. Had I mentioned this to her? I had not. I took it as a sign and said yes. We drove her Cherokee to a convention center in Wilmington. Gloria looked alive and trashy in a way that commanded attention but caused people to ask: did that just happen? Giant silver hoops in her ears, a low cut top, shorts so short she had to keep tugging to keep her cheeks in check. I placed my hand on her lower back, to let everyone know whose side I was on.

A laminated card reminded viewers these bodies were not the bodies of executed Chinese prisoners, as some had apparently claimed. They did all have something in common however, in that each one lacked flesh. Their musculature had been stripped away, in some cases flayed. I remembered a dream where I died but the electricity stayed on in my brain. No body movements, eyes open, staring at what was in front of me. I imagined every body here cursed with a similar power. Bodies dead, brains alive, flickering with a lesser consciousness, a perpetual state of perplexedness.

"My God," Gloria said to the flesh of an obese cadaver, which had been sliced into three sections to illustrate how fat was stored.

A woman in front of us, wearing a fanny pack, pointed to the ceiling, where a fleshless, bug-eyed woman with outstretched arms levitated. With my eyes on her teats—two blind and withered globes—I nearly tripped over another of the skinless bastards. It took me a second to figure out he was kneeling in prayer. He held his heart—or maybe somebody else's—in his hands. "Promise me something," I said.

"Shoot," Gloria replied.

"If I die in the next ten minutes, have me burned to a crisp. Fertilize your garden. Line your bird cages."

"Please."

"I suppose you'd prefer me to get all dolled up, stuff me into a box?"

"I'd prefer you to be eaten," she said. She grabbed my hand, started gnawing an index finger.

"I don't expect you'd like my taste."

"Not by me, retardo," she said. "Birds."

"Yours?"

She shook her head. "Too finicky. Turkey vultures, though? Turkey vultures would get the job done."

I took a break from the exhibit to conjure a vulture beak.

It scooped out one of Gloria's eyeballs.

"You okay?"

I wasn't sure. I felt like I had somewhere to get to, someplace I didn't want to visit. I pointed to her purse. "You got any booze in that thing?"

"You want a Midol?"

"I'm not menstruating."

She pressed the back of her hand to my forehead, pronounced it clammy.

"I could really use a drink."

"Take deep breaths," she said. "Close your eyes."

I nodded.

"Think about something nice."

My daughter appeared. She was a baby, maybe four. She was asking me how much I loved her. This was a game of ours. A pastime. She'd ask how much, I'd yell, "A gazillion!" I'd ask her how much she loved me and she'd yell, "Sixty!" "Wow," I'd say, "sixty's a lot."

"Is sixty a lot?" I ask.

"It depends."

"Wrong," I say. I swallow. The back of my throat tastes like snot. "Sixty's not a lot. Sixty's nothing. I'm ten years from sixty now. That's nearly six times the number of years my daughter breathed the air of this earth before she was slain."

I hadn't meant to include this part. But I'd been staring at the muscle threads of a man carrying his own skin—like a coat—over his arm, and my mouth, as usual, had a mind of its own.

Halfway through the exhibit, Gloria and I found an oasis: a bamboo café. At the counter, an adolescent boy with a Mohawk dispensed coffee and offered us free chunks of nut-infested brownies. We sat at a wobbly table, its unwiped surface agleam with the residue of spilled beverages. I took one sip and scalded my tongue. The story arrived like a deluge.

Once upon a time, a man and a woman made a child. The child wasn't perfect. In fact, the child was, for the first two years of her life, a terror. Never satisfied, threw tantrums, the whole bit. Toddlerhood, however, transformed her. She learned how to speak. She didn't lose the mean-spiritedness, which she'd inherited from her father, but she loved to talk, to tell her parents how much she loved them. She loved to love, loved to be loved. She'd don her Snow White mask, listen to the man's heartbeat through a fake stethoscope, shake her head gravely, and say: "You haven't had enough kisses today."

One day, another man—a neighbor, no less—had invited this child into his truck. Something had happened to her parents, he'd told her. But nothing had. What'd happened was he had dreamed of performing unspeakable acts upon the girl's body, before her death, and after. And that's what he did. Six days went by. On the seventh, a fisherman found the girl's hand bobbing in a river. Cops and parents were summoned, the body was identified, the predator nabbed, the funeral performed and forgotten.

In the years that followed, the woman was the one who proved herself. She wept often, but not always. She slept at night, got up in the morning. She found ways to go on, move on, get past, overcome. Meanwhile, the man lay in bed, grinding his teeth like he had a mouthful of glass. She'd tell him to go on, and he'd go on, out somewhere, into whatever building had its doors open and encouraged the worst habits money could buy. Eventually, the woman moved west with an aspiring soul winner, sent postcards from the desert imploring her ex to get personal with the Lord. For a while, the man did get personal. He cussed the Lord like you would a family member. Then, one day, the Lord broke the news: a daughter who'd been hacked to pulp couldn't be buried. He would carry the pulp with him. That pulp was hi heart. It would lend no hand with sympathy.

It wouldn't let him die.

Gloria's fingers—her talon-like nails shellacked with paint—fanned her eyes, as if casting a spell on her face. Her lips turned inward.

"Don't," I said, "You're not pretty when you cry."

"Baby," she replied. "Don't be mean."

"I'd have to die first," I said.

Gloria put her lips to my ear. "I want you inside me."

"I'll allow it," I whispered, "on one condition."

"Anything," she said.

"No matter what transpires, you won't shed a tear."

She said she'd promise me nothing. I knew then she was mine.

We had a whole floor to get through—bodies playing poker but not, bodies running but not, bodies conducting an orchestra and posing like the Thinker and riding flesh-stripped bodies of horses but not—and then, after the exit, the harsh light of a downsloping sun. How much of us would it fail to reveal? Only time would tell. Right now we had bodies to view, some whole, some not, some torn down the middle. We had bloated hearts and charred lungs and shriveled peckers to size up. We had shudders to inhabit. We had conversations to overhear: my uncle had heart disease; epidermis is your largest organ; I knew someone with a hydrocephalic child; I happen to think we'd be beautiful without skin!

I looked for the girl I'd seen before, the one who looked like my daughter. I told Gloria what she looked like, told her to alert me should one like her make an appearance. Look out for braids, I said. Strawberry-colored barrettes. Baby fat. Brown limbs and crooked teeth. A propensity to rely on fingers when counting. An insatiable love for animals, especially those injured, made lame, or missing a leg.

I had no reason to dream. I had no business envisioning a new era, where everything vital would come back from the dead. But, I told myself, I was keeping my eyes open. Peeled, as they say.

But back at her apartment, Gloria wanted them shut. She had a present for me, and this present required a blindfold. I lay prostate-side-up on her floor, like she asked. Also: my clothes were gone, removed by Gloria herself. I was a little afraid, and said so.

"Don't be," Gloria said. I heard bird peeps, the squeak of cage doors flung open. "Relax," she said.

"Impossible," I replied.

"Then pretend. Pretend like you know how to relax."

"Play dead?"

"Exactly."

Soon they were upon me. Their tiny bird feet. Their claws. Their beaks, nibbling and nibbling. The little wings, feather-kissing my flesh.

"Move your hands," Gloria said.

"I wish for that part of me to remain unpecked," I said.

"Leave that to me," she said. She climbed aboard.

The birds tweeted. One nipped at my ear, another at the

cloth above my eyelid. Gloria rocked and rocked.

"Are we…too old…for babies?" I asked.

"Let me…get back to you…"

"Keep…getting…back."

"Keep…inquiring."

I inquired.

The air pulsed with bird wings. I hadn't known she had so many. Maybe they weren't all hers. Maybe they'd flown through the open windows, from all directions—from the land, from the trees, the sky, the sea. The screeches they made! A cacophonous song—one that, I suspected, was imploring their winged brethren to abandon the dead and rotting things of the world, so as to observe our fervent wallowing. We were, I was sure, a sight to behold: two withered creatures, laboring and laboring, blind with the belief we might make something new.

WILL & TESTAMENT

October 30, 2001

To Whom It May Concern:

Enclosed please find the last will and testament of Andrew Walter[1], which, as of five-thirty p.m. today, will be simultaneously submitted to twenty-seven unknown readers, in the hopes that one of them might accept the role of executor[2].

To choose these persons, the undersigned, with the help of the Manhattan Phone Book, recited the names and addresses of possible candidates aloud. Candidates were chosen partly because of the aural pleasure obtained by reciting their names and addresses, and partly because the visions that unspooled during this recitation were harmonious with the undersigned's idea of the kind of person the executor should be—i.e., someone sympathetic enough to stop when passing the injured, yet not sentimental enough to think herself/himself a hero; someone intelligent enough to complete a *New York Times* crossword puzzle, yet humble enough to say it was just a thing they did while waiting for the next thing to happen; someone might pause—on a train, under a bridge, on a toilet—to read, and perhaps memorize, an extraordinary graffiti passage.

The undersigned acknowledges these unreliable methods

---

1 By the time the reader receives these documents, the undersigned will have already have been dead for some hours. Though the undersigned has taken some necessary precautions to prevent body spoilage, the reader should act quickly so that the last wishes of the undersigned might be met.
2 The undersigned has decided to eschew the tradition of referring to a female executor as "executrix." Therefore, as the undersigned uses it, "executor" should remain neutral.

might have led him to make inappropriate choices. Indeed, some recipients may find the following subject matter[3] offensive, and may conclude that the undersigned is insane, blasphemous, or perverted. In this event, the undersigned apologizes, and asks that the recipient destroy these documents.

Though the letters of the undersigned's name will, undoubtedly, have a particular effect upon the reader—an association produced by the particular combination of the letters, conjuring up a vision, however irrational, however unclear, of what the undersigned might look like —the undersigned understands that the reader will have not known him. The undersigned has figured, based on the proximity of the address, as well as the undersigned's affinity for brisk walks, that there is a very good possibility that he has passed the reader in the street—though the undersigned's face was, most likely, simply another face in that churning face-mass each day brings, and so the undersigned's face probably tumbled, along with the hundreds of other faces of the day, down the laundry chute of the reader's head into oblivion or, if the undersigned was lucky, into that unconscious well where he might be drawn up, momentarily, in a dream. Perhaps, as he types, the undersigned is performing any number of things, without his consent, in the confines of other people's heads,

---

3 The reader should also know that the undersigned is composing this in between answering phones, making copies, addressing envelopes, and entering data concerning the promotional materials of the A.J. Forsythe investment firm, and while the cube in which he works seems an appropriate environment for the last day of his life (photos of a dog, a boy, and a party which are not his, a half-eaten chocolate bunny in the top desk drawer, and a placard, slapped on the forehead of his monitor, that reads SPOILED ROTTEN!), it is not the best environment in which to compose, and the document may be riddled with errors and inaccuracies. Hence, the undersigned begs the reader's pardon should these last wishes be untranslatable.

though it's more likely, since he has a face that he's been forced, at times, to repress, that he's been forgotten altogether. It is not, however, the undersigned's intent to create a sense of guilt[4] in the reader for his/her failure to remember the undersigned's face. In fact, anonymity is of the utmost importance for the undersigned, as his purpose is to allow the reader, should the reader so desire, to believe that Fate has had a hand in the proceedings. Though the undersigned does not believe, necessarily, in Providence, he believes that this somewhat random act of choosing potential executors will allow s/he who decides to follow the accompanying procedures to indulge a sensation of having been chosen, thus granting said procedures a significance that they might not have otherwise possessed.

That said, the undersigned asks that the recipient of these documents, in a spirit of goodwill, consider following the procedures set forth in the accompanying will and testament, in an effort to help keep the undersigned's memory, or what's left of it, alive.

Signed, this 30th Day of October, 2001.

_____

Andrew Walter

LAST WILL AND TESTAMENT OF ANDREW WALTER

I.

The undersigned, Andrew Walter, residing at 12A Lazarus Court, Brooklyn, New York, being of sound mind and body, does hereby declare this instrument to be his last will and testament.

---

4 Guilt, the undersigned believes, is for the damned.

II.
The undersigned hereby revokes all previous wills and codicils.

III.
The undersigned hereby directs that the disposition of his remains be as follows:

A. ACQUIRING THE BODY:
At Terminal D of the LaGuardia Airport, across from a newsstand, stands a locker numbered 15B, combination 5-25-74. In this locker the executor will find a key to the undersigned's apartment, directions for acquiring the body of the deceased (the location of which, by this point, will have remained unknown), as well as access codes to a bank account containing the undersigned's life savings, which should be used for any expenses accrued in the distribution of both the undersigned's body and his possessions. Leftover monies should be accepted by the executor as payment for her/his participation.

B. WHAT MIGHT BE DONE WITH THE BODY:
Once contacted by the executor, the undersigned's neighbor, a Mr. Charles Christopher—having assured the undersigned that his thirteen months at Johns Hopkins Medical School granted him more than sufficient knowledge concerning the dissection of human cadavers—has agreed, in lieu of the traditional embalming, to perform the favor of separating skull, skeleton, body fat, brain, and heart from the remainder of the deceased's body. Fat, brain and heart will be placed immediately into plastic bags, then separate coolers[5], until the

---

5 Executor will find supplies, as well as wardrobe (which can be either worn by executor or donated to Goodwill), in bedroom closet of the deceased.

respective parts are to be prepared and delivered to the destinations described below. In return, Mr. Christopher[6] will receive the undersigned's rare and highly valuable antique Ouija board (the details of which are spelled out in section IV-C of this document).

1. **Skull:** The undersigned would ask that his skull be given to one of the following doctors, providing said doctor place the skull upon a shelf in her/his office: Dr. Bill Jameson; Dr. Rachel Hawthorne; Drs. Lola and Marvin Randy; and Dr. Weston Hildebrand. These physicians—all of whom the undersigned has visited at least three times in the last year—should be reminded that the deceased's skull could serve several functions. One: a kind of model for understanding where scientists believe memory is located, as well as various points of entry, and Two: when hinges are attached to the jaw, the skull might provide its owner with a macabre, though humorous, puppet. "Mr. Bones" might teach otherwise skeptical children the importance of abstaining from flesh foods, flossing after every meal, washing one's hands regularly to prevent the spread of disease, and drinking plenty of fluids.
2. **Remainder of Skeleton:** The undersigned has made arrangements[7] with a progressive elementary school, St.

---

6 In the event that Mr. Charles Christopher refuses to make good on his word, the deceased's body, fully intact, should be delivered to the nearest medical-research facility. In this case, Mr. Christopher shall not receive said antique Ouija board, regardless of how much begging Mr. Christopher performs, and the board shall be ceremoniously set aflame.

7 "Arrangements" here simply means that the undersigned spoke with the biology teacher, Mr. Eric Yancey, who led the undersigned to believe that, after death, his bones would be welcome, if they were thoroughly sanitized and disinfected—though he could make no promises.

Enid's, on the Upper West Side, that will accept his skeleton. The skeleton could be hung on the wall of their biology lab, as both model of the human body and, hopefully, as a reminder of what students will someday be reduced to. (The undersigned hopes that this reminder of one's brief passage through this earthly realm will encourage students to treasure each unthinkable moment of their lives, though he recognizes that the sight of his bones might contribute to some kind of death desensitization, which may or may not be so bad, depending on one's mental disposition and/or metaphysics.)

3.   **Fat:** Body fat should be removed from the remains of the deceased and placed inside a cooler, which should then be delivered to lamp maker Gabrielle Whiting, who works in a loft above a buffet in Chinatown, and with whom discreet arrangements have already been made to use the undersigned's fat, not unlike the versatile blubber of the whale, as fuel for light. The undersigned has estimated[8] that he has fat enough for ten lamps, to be distributed to the following ten women the undersigned has thought of, at some time or other, as his friends, some of whom he had dreamed, however fantastically, of loving: Hope Ramsey, Paris Kim, Lydia Gonzalez, Whitney Silvers, Anjeannette LaRoche, Raquel Davis, Daphne Finch, Jill Loganberry, Julie Smith, and Penelope Jones[9]. For the sake of their delicate sensibilities, recipi-

8 See schematic no. 1 on page 2 of a notebook, which will hereafter be referred to as the "Appendix," and which can be found inside the aforementioned locker in Terminal D of the LaGuardia Airport.
9 The addresses of these women, who have most likely forgotten the undersigned, are available on page 3 of the Appendix.

ents of the lamps should not be told how the lamps are fueled. They need know only that the undersigned wishes to provide them with the kind of light in which their ancestors worked—the unstable and dramatic flickering of the lamp, the kind of light in which so many of us look best.

4.   **Brain:** The brain of the undersigned shall be sliced, by Mr. Charles Christopher, into sixty-six rectangular pieces—the exact number of companies/organizations the undersigned worked for during his life. These pieces of the undersigned's brain shall be placed, along with a splash of formaldehyde, into clear glass vials, each of which shall then be corked, labeled, packed tightly in green shipping peanuts, and hand-delivered in a watch-case-sized box to the CEOs/ presidents of these companies/ organizations[10]. The following note should accompany each vial: Dear Sir/Madam; Here is a little something to remember me by. Enjoyed (circle all that apply): making copies/entering data/manning desk/   folding pam-phlets/surfing Internet at your top-notch company and/or organization. Adieu, AW.

5.   **Heart:** The undersigned's heart should be removed, wrapped in plastic, packed in a small cooler of dry ice, placed in a square pinewood box[11], and shipped to eastern Tennessee, where the undersigned's cousin, Marty

---

10 Names and addresses of said companies available on page 6 of Appendix. Vials can be found in the fridge of the undersigned's apartment.
11This box, measuring 8 x 8 inches, which he purchased for an unbeatable price at Box Town, can be found in the top cupboard of the undersigned's apartment, above the stove on the right-hand side.

Richards, maintains a plot of ground behind his A-frame in which deceased members of the Walter family, including the parents of the undersigned, have been laid to rest. No marked headstone is required, though the executor might mention to Mr. Richards that a jagged rock, rolled up from a creek bed, and stood, pointy part up, would be greatly appreciated.

6:   **Remainder of Body:** To be delivered by Mr. Charles Christopher to Abraham Crematorium.

IV. THE UNDERSIGNED'S POSSESSIONS:

A.   **Books:** The undersigned owns few books, since the majority have been accidentally left on the seats of subway trains and upon the pews of various cathedrals. The following are the ones he refuses to remove from the house, and thus, can be found upon his nightstand:

1. *Inner Experience*, by Georges Bataille; Tao Te Ching, by Lao Zu; The Diary of a Young Girl, by Anne Frank; Song of Myself, by Walt Whitman; and Tales of a Fourth-Grade Nothing, by Judy Blume, should, within a year following the undersigned's death, be de-paged and handed out as flyers to passersby in Times Square, preferably those just recently coming from or going to stand in front of NBC's Today show window.

2. *The Selected Poems of Robert Frost* should be delivered to Paris Kim, the round Korean woman who can recite "Stopping by Woods on a Snowy Evening" from memory, and who has, for nearly six years now, shampooed, cut, shaved, and styled the undersigned's hair at In Tri Cut, on Beaumont Street.

3. Holy Bible, King James Version, which bears the undersigned's name in gold print, should be delivered to Ms. Raquel Davis, with whom the undersigned worked for three days, filling a temporary secretarial position at St. John's Episcopal Church in SoHo. Ms. Davis—who, as far as the undersigned could tell, had been blessed not only with a striking, if not luminous, winter tan, but also a lovely speaking voice—might be asked to read the first chapter of St. John aloud. If Ms. Davis will allow it, her voice might also be recorded.[12] Also, if Ms. Davis would accept it, the Bible should be given to her. She may keep the photograph inside—a blurry image of the undersigned's father, Hal, with his second wife, Regan, which was sent to the undersigned during the couple's vacation to Iceland, days before the undersigned's father swallowed[13] forty-six sleeping pills, subsequently falling into a permanent slumber.

B. **Candles:** In an ideal world, every Friday, for twenty-seven minutes, for twenty-seven consecutive weeks—the exact number of years the undersigned spent on earth—one candle from the undersigned's handmade collection would be chosen and lit. At this time, the recorded voice of Ms. Raquel Davis's reading of the first chapter of St. John would be played. The undersigned realizes, however, that such a ritual may involve an unprecedented level of commitment from the executor. Therefore, if the executor lights a candle every once in a while, and remembers the undersigned for a moment, he would consider this request granted.

---

12 See Section IV. A, in which Ms. Davis's voice is put to good use.
13 Or was made to swallow, as the undersigned's sister is wont to believe.

C.   **Rare, Highly Valuable Antique Ouija Board:** The undersigned owns one antique Ouija board, reportedly used by his
great-grandmother Elsie to contact the spirit of Miles Whit-
comb Gardner, an eighteenth-century blacksmith to whom
she claimed to have been married in a previous life. Though
the undersigned, despite multiple attempts, has yet to receive
a response to what he believes are the simplest questions[14], the
aforementioned Mr. Charles Christopher seems to believe he
can make the board come alive. Should he fulfill his part of the
bargain (see section III), the board is his. If not, the board
should be, as stated earlier, ceremoniously set aflame.

D.   **Food:** All leftover food should either be consumed by
the executor, slowly and solemnly, in the light of one of the
aforementioned candles, or, if the executor feels uneasy about
consuming the food of a strange dead man, be broken up
into pieces and used to feed seagulls, pigeons, or the executor's favorite bird. Although the undersigned prefers a
winged creature, any living creature in need of nourishment
is acceptable.

E.   **LPs:** The undersigned's record collection, albeit quite in-
significant, should be delivered to Ms. Lydia Gonzalez, with
whom the undersigned spent one afternoon working at
www.bigdongs.com, the headquarters of which were composed of a gray, vaulted office space filled with a maze of
cubicles, all of which appeared to have been vacated except
for the undersigned's, whose job it was to divert the phone

---

14 E.g., does this tie match these slacks?, will it rain today?, and, will X call
me back?

calls of hostile "big dong" customers, and Lydia's, whose job it was, as far as the undersigned could tell, to answer a deluge of email while simultaneously providing a series of directives, via telephone, in Spanish. Though the undersigned was too timid to strike up a conversation, the rhythms of Ms. Gonzalez's fingers upon her keyboard and the untranslatable cadences that streamed, unbroken, from her mouth, formed a kind of music, and thus the undersigned feels, why not, she is entitled to his meager collection.[15]

F.   **Photographs:** Self-portraits of the undersigned should be either a) burned in one of the lamps whose fuel is his fat[16], or b) sent to people who share the same name[17], with a note explaining the following: *Dear Andrew Walter: We have spent a lifetime sharing the same name. People have shouted out our names and our heads have turned. Certainly, we would like to think, that there is something to this. Only we probably realize this is not the case. Please bask in the undeniable meaninglessness of this coincidence, and enjoy the picture. Sincerely, Andrew Walter.*

Photographs of the undersigned's acquaintances, though few and far between, should be sent to those friends[18], with this note attached: A hypothesis: *if one is forgotten enough times, one ceases to exist. Forgive me if my failure to remember your*

---

15 Ms. Gonzalez should know that, ideally, should she accept the collection, Dusty Springfield's Dusty in Memphis and Schubert's Winterreise might be played—alternately—on the thirtieth of October, the anniversary of the undersigned's death.

16 Obviously, this would be done before the lamps are delivered to the ten women.

17 The undersigned has kept a list of persons who share the same name, or a slight variation thereof. This list occurs on page 12 of the Appendix.

18 The names of the acquaintances appear on the backs of the photos. Addresses appear on page 13 of the Appendix.

face contributed to your gradual and inevitable annihilation. Yours, AW.

G. **"Faceless Man" painting:** An oil-painting of a man, minus face, sitting in a chair, reading a book beneath a willow tree, was composed by the undersigned's mother before he was born[19], and now hangs above the undersigned's sleeping mat in his apartment. The painting, as the executor will discover, appears at first glance to be unfinished. However, the undersigned likes to think of the painting as a completed work, and, more specifically, a portrait of the undersigned himself. Though the man in the painting is obviously in much better physical condition than the undersigned, the undersigned feels they have something in common, perhaps because the undersigned's older sister used to tell him that their mother had intended it to be a portrait of the undersigned himself—a kind of prediction of what he would look like once he grew up: someday, his face would simply disappear.

The painting should be delivered to a Ms. Penelope Jones, originally from Tallahassee, Florida, who works as a receptionist for Jacob and Jacob at 115 Houston Street. The undersigned spent two weeks under the tutelage of Ms. Jones, who, though six months pregnant, did an unparalleled job of showing the undersigned, who would perform all of Ms. Jones' secretarial duties during her maternity leave, the ropes.

As a way of explanation, a note might be delivered with the painting: *Dear Ms. Jones: I would probably never admit this if I*

---

19 The undersigned's mother, coincidentally, died of kidney failure before he was old enough to remember, in any organic way, her face.

didn't know you would never see me again. I have always felt, since the day you explained how to use the dictation machine, that in another life I would have liked to have been your baby, your son. I am not ashamed to say that I have imagined a life in which you were my mother: that you cradled me, packed my lunches, scrubbed my bloody elbows with hydrogen peroxide, picked me up in the van from my music lessons. Therefore, it is my wish that you would accept this painting, which was made by my own actual mother, whom I never knew. Yours sincerely, AW.

H. **Apartment:** The undersigned hereby declares that, assuming that the executor has completed the tasks described in this document, the apartment[20] shall become the sole property of the executor.

---

20 The apartment, though quite small, boasts a view of the avenue, and if the executor looks closely, s/he will find constellations of the undersigned's fingerprints upon the sliding glass door. Though the undersigned knows no view can save us (we must save ourselves, be saved by others, or, if the executor believes in God, be saved by her/his God), he endorses said window as a place for contemplation. In fact, the undersigned stood there when the idea of this will and testament struck him, just as he stood there when he opened the Manhattan phone book and began to recite the names of potential executors, and as he leaned his head against the cool pane, he imagined the potential executor entering the apartment. He imagined this executor startled by the lack of furniture, the sweet, slightly sour odor of garbage—imagined the executor drawn toward the portable radio beside the window, a radio which will have been purposely left on as a kind of hospitable gesture, a kind of "welcome home" for the executor. The executor, of course, can turn the radio off, as said radio will be, most likely, playing a song the executor has heard before. The undersigned expects that the executor is someone who, like himself, has heard it all. However, the undersigned hopes, and indeed believes, that the executor will keep on singing. The executor, he expects, will have a beautiful voice, as all voices are beautiful when singing—especially if they sing, as the undersigned thinks the executor might, slightly off-key. Perhaps, the undersigned thinks, he will hear this same voice when he descends this evening into the streets, on the way to his unmarked tomb, where his body will exhale its last breath and begin to fade.

FUTURE MISSIONARIES OF AMERICA

It's sleeting on Valentine's Day. I'm in the back booth of the Franklin Street McDonald's, waiting for Melashenko to deliver the robotic baby we're supposed to keep from suffering the slings and arrows of an unhappy infanthood, and writing him a letter on a napkin with the emergency topless ballpoint I keep in a hole in the lining of my hoodie. I write a I. in the corner of the first napkin and below that the date, *February 14, 2003*. I consider adding a little arrow-pierced heart, but I don't want to conjure even the smallest of question marks in Melashenko's head, so instead I draw a phantom heart in the air above the paper, which only confirms that I should definitely not draw it for real and that hearts are even more dangerous than sentimental closing signatures like *Love or Love ya* or *Yours*, any of which could inspire Melashenko to think I might think or even hope that we're anything more than we are. So, potentially disastrous heart drawing averted, I begin the letter, as usual, with *Dear Melashenko* (his first name's David but I use his last because I like the way it sounds, plus it ensures that I maintain a certain level of formality). Ten minutes later I've scribbled seven napkins' worth of words, which I roll into a floppy scroll. I snap a hair band around the middle and draw the letters of his name down the side in the Gothiest font I can muster, to give it this look like it might've been written by an ancient scribe, one who'd dreamed of future devastations and consigned them to this fragile parchment, to be delivered on this date to the father of a baby who's never been born.

Melashenko's been my project since French II. My job? To school him re *reality*. The first few weeks of class, we didn't talk, despite the fact that he sat right in front of me. I assumed that because he wore Izod and Polo and never once turned around to say bonjour that he was a stuck-up a-hole—a dude who had a Carolina-blue brick road paved straight to a frat-house date rape. When Madame Jacques called on him to recite dialogue, he pronounced every word in an impeccable French accent, which immediately made me think, okay, maybe he's gay. But one day, I arrived early to set up my class project (I was in charge of assembling an authentic French café, complete with a red and white checkered tablecloth, espresso, Nutella, baguettes, and a CD of accordion music) and there was Melashenko, in his regular seat, scribbling furiously on a semitransparent sheet of air mail stationery. I was like, What's the deal, are we writing letters to French kids now and he said, No, I'm writing to a friend in Ivory Coast, West Africa. No way, I said, that's cool, is the person African and if so how did you meet him and he said it's a she, her parents are missionaries, and I've been writing her for the past five years. He explained that his church had this magazine for kids called *Junior Guide* and that every week they listed the names of potential pen pals, along with their hobbies and interests, and when he saw that hers were horses and drawing and piano and pizza, and that she lived in Abidjan, he decided on a whim to write and then it was just like they hit it off as friends and have been exchanging one a week, which, he explained, is sometimes hard because you don't feel like you have much to say, but when that happens you just think up a string of weird and/or funny questions to ask.

This forced me to reconsider my initial assessment of Melashenko. Why would a religious dork spritzing himself with Drakkar Noir masquerade as a douche bag? What did he write in his letters? What did he receive? I needed an answer. So, during our next class period, as we suffered through another outdated *French in Action* video, I slid him a note of my own.

Me: *Hey, is Mirelle wearing a bra in this one?*

DM: *I haven't noticed.*

Me: *Yeah right.*

DM: *Okay maybe I did but I'm trying not to.*

Me: *Why would you be trying not to?*

DM: *I think about that kind of stuff enough as it is.*

Me: *What kind of stuff do you mean?*

DM: *You're familiar with the hormone testosterone?*

Me: *So what, you're trying to keep yourself from devolving into some kind of hornball? Isn't that inevitable?*

DM: *I hope not. It doesn't seem very becoming. Also doesn't exactly lead to the right kind of girls.*

Me: *What are the right kind?*

DM:*The kind that have respect for their bodies.*

Me: *Ah! You mean the kind that refuse themselves orgasms?!*

DM: *Okay ha ha not even going there.*

That exchange led to more note passing, which then led to a string, then a series, then a daily (sometimes twice and even thrice daily) exchange of fully developed letters, me asking Melashenko questions and Melashenko answering them, and then him asking me and me answering. His questions were often these improbable hypotheticals like:

DM: *You're floating on a raft in the middle of the ocean waiting to be rescued, what are you thinking about to pass the time?*

Me: *Morrissey lyrics, toast and jam, reruns of Bewitched.*

(or)

DM: *Your house is on fire what do you take with you?*

Me: *My oboe, my cat Percy, my Obscure Celebrity postcard collection.*

(or)

DM: *You get one question to ask God, what do you ask?*

Me: *What the hell were we supposed to learn from Hitler turning people into lampshades?*

My questions, however, were always more direct, more or less confrontational, like:

Me: *Aren't you even curious about the consciousness-raising properties of illicit drugs?*

DM: *Sure, but why trade the brain cells?*

(or)

Me: *What if Mirelle offered to blow you?*

DM: *Highly unlikely but if so despite everything I know in that situation I actually might have to cave.*

(or)

Me: *So what's up with this church of yours, the rebels of Christendom, who think they're too good to worship on Sunday?*

DM: *Remember when Adam and Eve ate the forbidden fruit and got kicked out of the garden forever? At that point, God could've snapped his fingers and said, Do over. But God isn't that kind of God. The kind of God He is, He lets people make bad decisions and still loves them after. It's like if you had a child would you force that child to love you? And if it didn't, would you kill it and create another one? Of course not. So imagine the love that you might have for that child and times it by like a billion. And that's not even close to how much God loves you. Once you realize this, you can't help but want to keep His commandments, one of which is, and you can look this up for yourself in Exodus 20:8-11, remember the seventh day to keep it holy).*

A few minutes after I've finished my letter, Melashenko arrives. He climbs out of his 1987 Reliant K (a boxy four-door that leans to the left and looks like it might be auditioning for a demolition derby) and fastens the buttons of his London Fog trench coat. Bareheaded, he turns toward the restaurant and squints, perhaps to prevent sleet from flying into his eyes. I slide down in my seat, hide behind a patch of condensation I've exhaled onto the glass, and through a peephole I create with my thumb I watch as Melashenko opens an umbrella then struggles to grip it underneath his chin. When that doesn't work, he stuffs it into an armpit so he can use two hands to open the back door and unlock the baby carrier.

From far away the baby—an infant simulator we've agreed to refer to as Beth, because Beth is a sweet and thus ridiculous name for what is essentially a machine—looks like an actual baby and up close it looks like a pretty amazing facsimile of an actual baby, which it is, but it's also much more than that, since not only does it cry and pee and drink and sleep and coo, but it will also eventually get plugged into a console, where it will transmit for Mrs. Jackson, our Health/Preg Ed teacher a record of everything we've done (and have neglected to do): in other words, which of us have shaken our babies or under- or overfed them or failed to change their diapers or ignored them or hung them upside down by their feet or allowed them to be submerged underwater or screamed at them or subjected them for dangerous periods of time to frigid temperatures.

As usual, Melashenko's looking spiffy (what with his trench and khakis and Gore-Tex boots and a pink Ralph Lauren oxford) and the sight of him, carrying the umbrella and Beth, who's heaped with blankets and sporting a winter hat with a pom-pom on top, launches a little flare of jealousy through my chest. Because no matter how much I resent Melashenko for being so unbelievably wholesome and making good grades and believing Jesus Christ is his personal savior and in general living a charmed life, I can't help but assume that his meticulousness in robot-baby rearing is actually a foreshadowing of what a good and kindhearted and selfless dad he will someday make, and that I, Alexandra Aileen Kurtis, will play little to no part in that experience. Unless, of course, he surprises me by keeping his promise to exchange letters from now until as long as we both shall live—a next-to-impossible feat, to be sure, but one that would guarantee that our voices would outlast our bodies, since what editor in his or her right mind would ever pass up a lifetime of private correspondence between two relentlessly charming and witty persons? It's really the only way we could ever hope to be united, assuming we'd ever hope that, which probably we wouldn't, since under no conditions would Melashenko allow himself to be unequally yoked, which means that he doesn't date, and certainly wouldn't marry, someone who isn't a baptized member of the Seventh-day Adventist Church. Not that I'd marry Melashenko; he's enough of a freak to drive even a robot baby bat-shit insane.

"Hey," he says, placing the baby carrier on the table. He's out of breath. His cheeks are flushed and glossy. They look like they've been smeared with Vaseline. His hair, which is parted neatly and looks, as it always does, freshly shorn, sparkles with bits of ice. But his eyes. His eyes look weary. Bloodshot.

I flick the napkin scroll across the table.

He retrieves but doesn't open it. It's one of our rules. No

reading letters in public. Especially not in front of the person who wrote it.

He grimaces. "I don't have one for you."

"That's okay," I say, shrugging to hide my disappointment. Another rule: write only when you feel compelled. An unspoken rule? Always feel compelled. "Obviously," I continue, "Beth has required all your attention."

"How'd you guess?"

"You look beleaguered," I say. "Like an actual father."

"I *feel* beleaguered," Melashenko says.

"Which is sort of the point, right?"

"Like if we realize how exhausting parenthood is, we won't have unprotected sex?"

"Yeah," I say. "Because sex is never spontaneous or unplanned."

Melashenko laughs. Melashenko doesn't have unprotected sex. Melashenko doesn't have unplanned sex. He doesn't have sex, period—and won't, not until his wedding night. He explained this a few months ago, in a letter he scribbled during Western Civ: *You know Solomon, right? The King with 700 wives who once solved a custody dispute by threatening to slice a baby in half? In Proverbs, he says, As a man thinketh in his heart, so he is. Meaning, no matter how good we act, no matter what we do or don't do, it's what's in our hearts that matters. And that's the problem. Everyone's heart is full of excrement. Mine, too. Even so, and maybe this makes me a dumb, naive romantic, but I want to say to the one I marry, I may not come to you whole, I may in fact come to you with a diseased heart, but this flesh, this is yours alone.*

"So, you want a sundae?" I say. "My treat."

"I don't know if I can," Melashenko says, checking his

watch, a silver Timex that he removes occasionally to wind. "I sort of have to get back. Mom's doing Valentine's dinner."

"Oh."

"You're disappointed."

"I'm not disappointed. I just thought if you wanted to meet at McDonald's you were thinking sundaes."

"You'd be more than welcome to join us."

"No thanks," I say. "I don't need a pity invitation."

"I figured you'd have a hot date."

"Yeah, me and the robot tot are going to paint the town fucking red."

Melashenko puts his hands on the sides of Beth's head. "She's got ears," he says.

I roll my eyes. "Isn't tonight your family's special night?" I know it is. I know that every Friday the Melashenkos gather together to light candles and pray and eat weird little Adventist suppers—veggie meat loaf, hot beans on bread sprinkled with Baco bits and smoke-flavored yeast, mushroom soup topped with almond slivers and whipped cream. But I don't want to seem like a stalker freak who remembers every little detail. Thus the faux uncertainty.

"Sure," he says. "But it's not just a family thing. We have people over all the time. Last week a choir from a boarding school in the Shenandoah Valley sang for church, and Mom invited the whole clan over afterwards. Thirty students we'd never even met before. I'm sure she can deal with one extra."

I pretend like I'm weighing my options. Should I take Beth the robot baby to a party where she'll be subjected to Linkin Park blasted from Ryan Hannigart's parents' stereo? Should I go home and listen to Mom bitch about all the papers she has to grade? Should I watch TV at Dad's while he tries to outbid some other overaged doofus for a Sarlaac Pit play set?

"Fine," I say. "I'll come. But we have to lay out some ground rules."

"Like what?"

"Like you have to step in if anybody tries to convert me."

Melashenko laughs. "Okay. No converting you."

"Also…thou shalt not mention my religious beliefs."

"I didn't know you possessed any."

"For real."

"Okay."

"As far as you know, I'm like Baptist or something."

"Let's say Episcopal."

"Fine," I say, eyeing him suspiciously. "And also? This isn't a date."

"Why would it be a date?" Melashenko asks, unleashing a goofy smile.

"It wouldn't," I say. Though I have to admit: I would've got a kick out of him saying it was.

Melashenko's old-school. Not old-school rap. More like old-school prep. He favors blue blazers and Top-Siders, has been known on special occasions to bust out a bow tie. He writes everything in pencil (the kind that requires sharpening), types on a Smith-Corona he bought for two bucks at a yard sale. Doesn't use microwaves (doesn't believe in them), guesses there might be something to reports linking cell phones to cancer. Computers, he thinks, are not only over-rated (the kind of technology that fools people into thinking they're saving time when they're actually wasting it), but are also probably going to play a key role in precipitating end time events, just as they did in the time of Noah *(No reason to think, he once wrote, that the antediluvian world wasn't as technologically advanced as our own).* Melashenko's favorite music, aside from baroque classical, is Delta blues, though a few weeks ago he started feeling guilty (what with those world-weary singers glorifying whores and whiskey) and burned all his LPs (yes, actual *records*), then a week later went back to the Skylight Exchange and started buying new ones, most likely with cash, since he won't use a debit card, not that it's the mark of the beast or anything, he just prefers bills in his wallet and a handful of change in his pocket, always a few quarters, in case he needs to make a call. Which he does now, from a pay phone outside McDonald's.

I rock Beth in my arms, and remembering that she's out-fitted not only with voice-detection technology but also a sensor that records how often she hears human voices, I explain, "Daddy will be back in a second, he's just gone to ask permission for Mommy to come to dinner and to give his parents a heads up, to tell them that I'm a girl he knows from school who, despite her septum piercing and green finger-nails and a black hoodie emblazoned with a thousand skulls, is totally harmless." Beth's expression doesn't change, because her face is molded plastic, but she manages a faint guttural, a dissatisfied gurgle, as if to say, *Don't patronize me, bitch; you aren't my mom, my mom's a factory in China, and if you don't believe me, then kiss my ass, on the spot where they branded me with her name.*

Sleet's been falling since noon. Tree limbs, laden with glassy ice burdens, droop. Other cars have slowed to a crawl. Doesn't matter: Melashenko drives the K car like a bat out of hell. We cut under traffic lights seconds after they turn red. We churn slush. We fishtail. We merge onto 15/501 and practically run a dude on a moped off the road. Reckless driving—it's one of

Melashenko's few vices, along with *Terminator* movies, an obsession with the Washington Redskins, beef nachos (his whole family's vegetarian), and, when he's feeling really wild, supermodels in sheer bikinis (Melashenko once confessed that, when he was thirteen, he'd walked into a Waldenbooks and purchased what we'd later refer to as a smutwich, which is when you sandwich a magazine of questionable repute—in this case, a *Sports Illustrated* swimsuit issue—between a Newsweek and a People, as if to suggest to the cashier that you're not only a beater of meat, you also keep tabs on current events and celebrity gossip).

"I'm not scaring you, am I?" Melashenko asks.

"No," I say, forcing a smile.

"You look sort of tense."

"I'm fine," I say.

"Why don't you read that letter to me?"

"Because that's against the rules."

"Screw the rules," Melashenko says.

"Wow. Strong language, Shenky-poo."

"You're right," he says. "It's one of those words, like suck, that's crept into my vocabulary." He grins at me, fishing the napkin scroll out of his shirt pocket. "Sorry to offend your delicate sensibilities."

He drops the letter in my lap.

"This one was intended to be read silently," I say.

"I'm sure it'll hold up when read aloud," Melashenko says.

"There's not enough light."

He flips down my vanity mirror.

I take a deep breath. Once Melashenko gets something in his head, there's really no use arguing. He'll harass you until you relent. I unroll the scroll and begin:

I. February 14, 2003. Dear Melashenko, Happy V-Day! You know that I've always been forbidden to celebrate this holiday at my house because that would be worshipping at the altar of consumerism, so instead of tickling your funny bone with a dorky card written by some chump chained to a cubicle, I will tell you a story about a girl I know.

II. Once upon a time, there was a girl. The girl lived with her mother in an apartment that the girl's father paid for, despite the fact that the mother and father no longer lived together. Even so, the father was very much in love with the mother and for years he kept calling her, kept begging her to return.

III. The girl's mother, however, did not love the girl's father, and always said no. Or, almost always said no. Sometimes, because she liked to be wanted and more than that enjoyed having someone to torture, she said yes, which meant that, on occasion, the father would be allowed to drop by for an impromptu visit.

IV. On one of these nights when the father arrived, he brought a videocassette and a bag of popcorn for the girl, and after he set her down in front of the TV, he and the girl's mother retreated to the bedroom and closed the door. "Don't worry," her mother said, "we'll be right here, just yell if you need anything." But then the girl began to watch the movie, which was about a widowed mouse who was trying to defend her brood from a gang of evil rats, and because she was scared she went to the bedroom door to sound a cry for help.

V. At the door, the girl heard things that made her think just the opposite of what she'd been told, that her parents weren't there, that they had been replaced by something monstrous. It sounded to the girl as though someone was being eaten alive: the smacking of a mouth, a moan, and, every so often, a yelp. The girl had never prayed before but she decided now was the

time. Dear God, she prayed, please help. But the sounds con-
tinued. In the shadows, along the walls, she imagined she could
see them: a thousand rats, a pulsing mass of fur and fangs.

VI. The door didn't open until the next morning. When it
did, it revealed only one parent: her mother, whose glistening
mouth was smeared with red. She wanted to know why the girl
was still up and the girl said she was scared, she had wanted to
give her father a hug good night. The girl's mother said she had
no idea what the girl was talking about, that the father didn't
live with them anymore.

VII. "Don't be a baby," she said, when the girl began to
sniffle. "I don't want to see you shedding a single tear. Because
you know who can smell tears? Monsters. And you know what
happens when they do? They think: Some delicious little girl is
crying. So think about that before you cry." Which the girl did.
She thought about the tear-thirsty monsters and didn't cry. She
could be strong and she was. She didn't shed a single tear. She
saved up all her tears on the inside. Then one day she got so full
she rolled away and nobody saw her again. The End.

"Huh," Melashenko says. "Abrupt ending." I roll up the napkins, bind them, hold them between my index and middle
finger like a fat cigar. "Sad, too."

"Stories," I say, taking an imaginary puff, "are supposed
to be sad. All the good ones, at least."

Melashenko nods. "Do good ones also leave out people's
names?"

"Do names really matter?"

"It does if it's yours."

"Nobody said this was about me."

"But obviously it is."

"So if someone tells a story without names you automatically assume it's about the person who wrote it?"

"Well, isn't it?"

"You're missing the point."

"Which is?"

"Which is what would you say to that little girl if you could? 'Fear not, my child, the Lord is with you'?"

"Hey," he says, "if there's ever a time for prayer…"

"No, you're probably right. I could totally see God taking a break from ignoring cancer and bombs and burn victims and people who feed pancake mix to foster kids living in dungeons to help a girl who, the last time she did anything remotely spiritual, was to help another girl brand her right tit with a pentagram heated over a candle flame."

"See?" Melashenko says. "It *is* you."

Turns out the Melashenko house isn't afraid to be worldly; it's a freaking castle of brick and stone. It looks like something from a calendar by that painter-of-light dude, what with the icicles dangling from the eaves and the yellow windows and the smoke unfurling from the chimney. As we crunch across the frosted yard to the back (sleet sticking to the sleeves of my hoodie, branches clinking overhead) I send a mental message to Beth the robot baby, which is *Don't get too used to this, remember our final destination's Unit D, Apartment 16 at Ramsgate Apartments, a place that more or less reeks of cat piss, baba ghanoush, Folger's coffee, and (because Mom's the kind of person who says, "Everything in moderation") Mexican schwag.*

We wipe our feet on a welcome mat shaped like a bumblebee, cross the threshold into the Melashenko kitchen, a room of white and blue tile. There are bowls of unblemished fruit on the counter, stainless steel appliances, a windowsill where a collection of miniature carolers are frozen midsong. Melashenko's Mom, a big-time doc at the Carolina Med School, has hair the color of golden retriever fur and a slim figure and a roundish face that, with its bee-stung lips and high cheekbones, radiates youth and cheerfulness. When Melashenko introduces me, she sets down the cube of cheddar she's been shredding, wipes her hands on her apron, and greets me like I'm a bona fide celebrity, saying things like "So this is the mother of my grandbabydoll?" and "*So* nice to finally meet" and "We've heard so much about you!"

"You too," I say.

"Well," Dr. M says, nodding toward Beth, who is now gurgling in my arms, "you obviously have the magic touch. We all took turns trying to quiet that thing."

"Robot babies," I say, squeezing Beth a little harder, in the hopes that she'll unleash a yelp and relieve me from the idea that we've formed some sort of pretend mother-baby bond. "They're so unpredictable."

Dr. M clicks her tongue. "Can you *believe* the technology? When we were in school we had to carry an egg around for a week. If you broke it, you failed."

"The times," Melashenko says, "they are a-changin'."

I roll my eyes.

"Don't even *look* at the house," Dr. M says. "It's a wreck."

But of course I look and of course the house is not a wreck. Everything in the house—with its antique lamps with pull chains and shiny mahogany tables and straight-backed chairs and plush carpet and wooden bowls of potpourri— seems like it's waiting for photographers from *Southern Living* to arrive and begin shooting. In the den Melashenko introduces me to his father (a tall, lean man with a hair-sprayed do who insists that I please call him Pastor Mel) and his two sisters (Elizabeth, the older one, is sitting Indian-style on a bean-bag in front of the fireplace, while Marnie, a girl about seven, wearing a cowboy hat, braids her hair).

"Look," Elizabeth says, nodding toward the baby. "The doll stopped crying."

"Just wait," Melashenko says, giving me a wink. "She's saving up all her tears on the inside."

All during dinner, I think about how I might describe everything in a future letter to Melashenko, like *I can still remember that first time I visited your house, how your mom had those little individual heart-shaped crystal dishes filled with Valentine's candy and how the plates were pink and bordered with little hearts, and everybody had their own miniature saltshaker and a goblet filled with gold, sparkling cider. And how she cut up heart-shaped slices of homemade bread and I spread mine with mayonnaise and mouthed "Shut up" to you because I could see you smiling, knowing I was philosophically against mayonnaise and just using it to be polite and I was already feeling self-conscious assembling this concoction of bread and lentils and cheese and lettuce and tomatoes, partly because I was afraid I'd do something wrong and partly because I was also squeezing a robot baby between my knees, and telling myself, "Whatever you do, don't screw up, or you'll have to start over."*

Pastor Mel wants to know where I live and I say, "With my mom," and he says, "What does she do?" and I give him the easy answer, saying she teaches English at UNC. What I don't tell him is that she teaches four sections of freshman comp, and spends most of her time bitching about how idiotic their papers are and stressing about her dissertation and worrying about how much time she has left before people will think she's old, a state of mind that inspired her in recent years to leave her blouses halfway unbuttoned, in the hopes that some young buck will write, *Ms. Kurtis is a total MILF*, on her evals.

"What about Dad?" Pastor Mel says, meaning mine.

"He's an orthodontist," I say. Melashenko nods, gives me this look that involves turning his lips inside his mouth, an expression intended to transmit sympathy, since he knows I haven't spoken to my father ever since our ill-fated trip to the Goodwill in Raleigh, where, among the battered and bitten and sucked-upon toys, Dad found a mint Millennium Falcon, and when he hoisted it off the shelf, a voice behind us said, "Excuse me sir, we were about to purchase that." So we turned around and there was this woman with cornrows holding the hand of a little boy with wet-green eyes. Dad looked at the box and said, "I don't see a hold tag on it," and the lady said, "No, my son saw it and came to get me," to which Dad responded, "Well, I'm sorry about that." And she said, "I was here first" and "I'll pay you twice as much as it costs," but Dad just walked to the front, the woman mumbling obscenities while the kid wailed, and I was like, "Dad, you can't do this," but he did, then in the car he asked me how much I thought the ship would go for on eBay, "We're talking a mint-condition, complete Millennium Falcon, with fully intact lithographs, incredibly rare, since even any gently played-with one normally is missing the cockpit glass, so to find one that's basically perfect could bring five hundred dollars or more. Come on, pumpkin, you understand, right? We live in a land of plenty! That kid isn't going to suffer because he failed to get a toy spaceship. And if you think that he is, if you really think that's suffering, then you've got a lot to learn."

Pastor Mel hopes I've saved room for dessert, which prompts Marnie to inquire whether I like poop soup. I'm like, "No thanks!" Which delights Marnie to no end because poop soup is merely the Melashenko's whacky nickname for hot *fruit* soup, which I expect to hate but don't, since it's soft and sticky and sweet and topped with homemade whipped cream. I've never had the pleasure of consuming homemade whipped cream before and when I say so Dr. Melashenko proclaims this a tragedy and immediately scribbles the recipe down on a card for me. Then Pastor Mel wants to know if I'm opposed to joining them for family worship and because I have a habit of being ultra-polite to adults I say, "Not at all, that'd be nice," but then I glance at Melashenko, whose shrug seems to be communicating something like a comical whoops! And I shoot back a look like, *Dude, if these people pull some kind of Bible study-slash-altar call bullshit you are so dead.* But then family worship turns out to be much less of a hoot than I'd expected, since there's really not much to make fun of. Dr. M is an accomplished pianist and all of the Melashenko clan knows how to sing, so instead of feeling embarrassed for them, I clutch Beth and detect the onset of a mild depression, not because I don't know the song and have to move my lips as they sing, *As the deer panteth for the water, so my soul longeth after thee,* but because I feel like the Melashenkos have created a family unit that, like a star, generates its own light and heat, and me, I'm merely an asteroid passing by, warmed for a moment before I reenter darkness.

We're on the fourth verse when we hear an explosion. Everybody runs to the window. Pastor Mel flips on the porch lights. Half of one of the trees in the backyard, its branches sheathed in ice, has toppled. Chunks of ice litter the grass. It looks like there might've been a yard sale for someone's crystal and someone else came along and bashed it to smithereens.

"I loved that tree," Elizabeth says.

"*I* loved that tree," Marnie says.

"Probably got about half an hour before the power goes out," Pastor Mel says.

"Better recharge the baby before it's too late," Dr. M says.

"Actually," I say, thinking I shouldn't put anybody out, "I should probably get going."

"Um," Melashenko says, "I don't think anybody'll be going out in this."

"You're snowed in!" Marnie exclaims.

"More like iced in," Elizabeth says.

"You're welcome to stay over," Dr. Melashenko says. "As long as your parents are okay with it."

I slide out my cell. It's dead. I pick up a yellow rotary in the kitchen and dial Mom. What is she doing? Getting her *American Idol* on, depleting her stack of papers by about one per hour, getting ready (maybe, she says, this is a big maybe) to take a little toot of something, just to, you know, get through the evening. And I'm like, "You've got blow?"

"A tiny bit," she says. "Almost nothing. Your father tracked it down for me; you know he's nothing if not connected. What in the world are *you* doing?"

"I'm on a hot date," I say, at the Melashenko's.

"The Mela-whos?"

"You know," I say, my robot-baby partner from school."

"Oh," she says, "so you made it into the inner sanctum? If you see any altars anywhere, run."

"Mom," I say, "please. It's not that kind of thing."

"Whatever," she says.

"Don't wait up," I say.

"Don't get sacrificed," she says.

In the living room, Marnie's explaining the rules to Chinese checkers—first you do this and then you do that and then whoever makes it to the other side wins—which leads Dr. M to tell a story about one of her patients who, after every sentence she utters, tallies its Scrabble word score. Elizabeth says that reminds her, she recently found this awesome Scrabble website, so that after David leaves they can all play online.

"Where are you going?" I ask.

Pastor Mel frowns. "You haven't told her?"

Melashenko recrosses his legs. "Ivory Coast," he says. "Africa."

"*Africa* Africa?" I say. "When?"

"After graduation," he says, "I'm flying to Abidjan. One of our schools there needs someone to teach English and Bible and—"

"Wait," I say, "how long have you known about this?"

"I don't know. Since Christmas?"

Pastor Mel grips the arms of his rocking chair, like he's preparing for liftoff.

"I was going to tell you," Melashenko says.

Going to tell me? I think. This doesn't seem like Melashenko. Not at all. I wonder, for a second, if maybe this might be a Melashenko imposter, if any second he'll pull on his hair and lift up a mask to reveal who he really is. Because the Melashenko I know? He tells me everything. If he spends his tithe on a bottle of cologne, if he buys a pack of cigarettes but ditches them before he has the courage to light one, if he goes to the video store to retrieve a copy of *Old Yeller* for Family Night but instead ends up reading and rereading the back of a video box for *Emmanuelle 4*, in which a woman transforms herself into a twenty-year-old virgin and then takes on the whole of Brazil in a series of sexual escapades, he tells me. I would very much enjoy reminding him of this, but I know he already knows it, is probably already writing a letter of apology in his head.

"No offense," I say, "but if I were going to Africa the whole effing world would know about it."

"What does *effing* mean?" Marnie says.

"It's a euphemism," her mother explains.

"What's a euphemism?"

"It's a stand-in word for an icky word."

"What's the icky word?"

"You don't need to know," Pastor Mel says.

Marnie huffs. "I always don't need to know."

"Ivory Coast," I say. "Isn't that where whatshername lives?"

I know her name. I just want to make him say it.

"You mean Harriet?"

"Yeah," I say. "Her."

Melashenko shrugs, like it's no big deal. "Yeah. It was her father who got me the position."

Dr. M must feel the tension in the room because she stands up and says brightly, "I think it's somebody's bedtime."

Marnie stamps her foot. "But I didn't get to play Baby Moses yet!"

Dr. M isn't sure if they should do Baby Moses tonight but Marnie begs and pleads and Dr. M caves saying, "You'll have to ask Alex, it's her baby," so Marnie says, "Alex, may we use Beth to play Baby Moses?" and I say, "Sure," because I could care less what they do with the baby at this point, they could play Solomon and slice it in half for all I care. Marnie disappears for a second and Melashenko raises his eyebrows at me and I glare at him, then stare at a magazine on the coffee table with the title *Signs of the Times*. On the cover there's a man with a white beard and long white hair hovering in space. In the background a bride in a gown waits on the moon. A boa-sized serpent with the head of a dragon wraps its crimson scales around the man's leg. The man has a sword and a cape and a square plate of jewels on his chest. The expression on his face looks exactly how I feel. Like he means business. *Dear Melashenko,* I think. *You suck.*

I do not like Harriet Kramer. I don't know that much about her, but I do know this: she's a happy, well-adjusted perfectionist. You can tell by looking at her handwriting. Melashenko's let me read a few of her letters, and her script (perfect cursive) lopes across the page, elegant and unadorned, a pleasure to read. I imagine the writing's a reflection of Harriet herself, and though I've never seen a photograph, despite the fact that Melashenko tried to show me one he keeps in his wallet (where he stores a whole collection of friends he's met at Adventist camporees and summer schools and Bible conferences), I already have a picture of her in my head: blond hair streaked with gold, skin that glows, a plain-looking face that's somehow stunning. Her letters? They're jam-packed with info, taking for granted that anyone would care, and the truth is most people would: stuff about how their guard, Muhammad, who's got six kids and three wives, once chopped a black mamba to bloody chunklets in their yard; how their chef, Ishmael, makes the most amazing *pomme frites*; how they went to a remote church where the children ran beside their van when they arrived and at the pot luck a guy popped the caps off Fanta bottles with his teeth; how you have to iron every article of clothing, including underwear, to kill the fly eggs; how you can't get a jar of peanut butter anywhere and she's dying for some; how she bought him the coolest knife at a place called Treshville, which is an open-air market where they sell horses' heads and when people buy meat there the butcher stuffs it into an ox stomach for them to use as a bag; how when you drive to the beach where ladies don't bother with tops you get past road-blocks by bribing the guards with church brochures, which says something about the people's needs there—they're so poor that they mistake the bright colors and glossy sheen of church pamphlets for something that might be worth something.

After the Baby Moses thing, which is essentially Marnie in a bathrobe, with a towel roped to her head, putting Beth the robot baby into a picnic basket and hiding it behind a potted fern (i.e., make-believe bulrushes) while Elizabeth pretends to be Pharaoh's daughter who finds him when she comes to bathe in the Nile, Dr. M makes me a bed on the couch, with sheets and an old quilt patched together by her grand-mother—a cloth whose weight reminds me of the lead apron you wear for X-rays at the dentist. Elizabeth donates an old Tar Heels T-shirt, apologizes for the Popsicle stains. Marnie can't part with her stuffed frog, Froggy, so instead she relin-quishes a rooster named Ernie. Melashenko wants to know if I really do want to take the baby for the night and I say as snippily as possible, "It's my child too. Are you questioning my motherhood?" And he laughs weakly and says, "Of course not, just wanted to make sure." Then he waves goodnight and I'm alone.

As the falling sleet ticks against the windows, I try to take Dad's advice for getting to sleep, which is to think of some-thing you'd love to do, something impossible, even, because good thoughts are soil for good dreams. With this in mind, I imagine the Melashenko house is a ship and we're embarking upon a perilous journey across an icy sea, beyond which lie the sugary shores of some secret island, where the plant leaves are fleshy and green and there are no natives, just us and birds with fantastic plumage and maybe some species of fun-loving monkey, but then, because I can only imagine wonderful things for so long, I imagine I hear something rattling below the deck and because I can't ignore rattling I open a hatch, peer into the darkness and realize that the room beneath us is chock-full of robot-baby stowaways. I expect them to shriek, to let loose a wail of recorded baby cries, but they don't. Then I realize: these are the dead ones—the ones whose parents failed them. The ones nobody could even pretend to love.

In the kitchen, I find a pad of paper advertising Ambien, the irony of which, as I begin writing, does not escape me, but I don't mention it, because this isn't going to be that kind of letter. The kind of letter I'm writing now I can't even write. Each time I start, I stop. I crumple up page after page, using half the pad. I try to get Beth back to sleep but she cries every time I lay her in her car seat, which Mrs. Jackson has said is a perfectly fine place for babies to sleep, as her own son spent his first month sleeping in his.

Eventually, I give up. I address the baby, saying, "What is it you want?" And though the baby doesn't speak, an answer appears in my head, as though using some combination of voice detection and a thought transmitter, she beamed it there: To be known.

"But you're not even real," I whisper. "You've been living a lie."

These words, entering her via a receiver hole the size of

a pinprick in her fake ear, apparently land on a sensitive spot in her microchips, because as soon as I lay her down, the sound of a baby crying—a baby experiencing a very special type of discomfort—erupts from the place inside her where the recordings of real babies have been stored, and for the first time I understand what Mrs. Jackson told us on the day when she unlocked the baby cabinet and activated each one and passed them out, which was that a baby in distress is one of the most anxiety-producing sounds a human can hear.

As I press her to my chest, I wonder if it's possible that there's something about Beth the robot baby that likes me best, if the particular rhythms of my body—imperceptible to me, singsongy to her—are, even now, transferring some essential information from me to her. "Don't even think about getting attached," I say. Because next week it'll be back to the baby cabinet, where she'll sleep the sleep of dead robot babies, waiting to be resurrected, to create a new turbulence in some other idiot teenager's life.

Upstairs, I creep down the hallway that leads to the Melashenkos' bedrooms, praying that Beth won't erupt into a preprogrammed fit. My goal? Find Melashenko, give him a piece of my mind. I peek into rooms lit by orangey nightlights, guess his isn't the one with the frog bedspread or the pages of bare-chested hunks pasted to the wall. At the end of the hall, there's a closed door and a slat of yellow light. I twist the handle, hoping I won't walk in on the Doc and Pastor Mel going at it doggy-style (*What, you thought we'd do it missionary?*), but there's Melashenko on his top bunk, wearing button-up flannel pajamas and holding a notebook and pen.

My eyes dart around the room. There's a *National Geographic* map of the United States on one wall, a glossy 8 x 10 of the Orion Nebula, several drawings of a Washington Redskins quarterback wearing an old-school one-bar helmet, a biography of Muddy Waters on top of his typewriter, and an aquarium where the faces of exotic fish—like wide-eyed, unblinking alien angels—register permanent astonishment.

"You okay?" Melashenko says.

"Can't sleep," I say.

"Me either."

"We need to talk."

"I know."

I hug Beth tight. I grip a rung on the ladder. "I'm coming up," I say.

Melashenko raises his eyebrows. "Okay," he says.

Melashenko's bed, I think. I am climbing onto Melashenko's *bed*. Who knows what dreams have transpired here, what longings, what glorious—and perhaps nightmarish—nocturnal emissions? How many delirious prayers have blasted off from this launch pad? How many hours spent begging for the strength not to touch himself, then touching himself?

"You're going to Africa," I say.

"I am."

"It never occurred to you to tell me?"

"I was going to tell you a lot of times. But I didn't know how."

"You could've used your mouth. Or even a pen. You have great penmanship skills."

"I didn't expect you'd be very supportive of the idea."

"I'm supportive. I can be supportive."

"Actually, I figured you'd probably write a story about some idealistic kid with big dreams who wants to change a world that'll never change."

"Why would I do that? I believe in change."

"Or that you'd think I was going because of Harriet."

"Why would I give a damn about Harriet?"

"See? You can't even talk about her without cursing."

The heat cuts off. The room is silent. Outside, the world is frozen. No wind. No creaking branches. My arm's touching Melashenko's arm. He's warm. I've never touched his bare flesh before. No part of him.

"I completely understand," I say. "You've jungles to traverse. Jeeps to ride. Brochures to distribute. Mothers of robot babies to abandon. All of which is a small price to pay for the winning of souls, right, little Beth!"

Beth squeaks. She hiccups. I spin her around, pat her back.

"Alex," he says. "It's not about winning souls. Honestly, I don't even know if it's about God. Right now it's about me. About me wanting to know who I'll be once I get there."

A vision unfurls inside my head: Melashenko riding an elephant, Melashenko handing out Bibles to Africans with golden bracelets orbiting their elongated necks like so many metal halos, Melashenko on his knees while a witch doctor shakes tufted sticks above his head, Melashenko dunking people in robes beneath the surface of a dirty river. How many days, I wonder, does it take a letter to reach Africa? I begin calculating—one day from Chapel Hill to Raleigh, another from Raleigh to New York, then on to Paris—but then the hot stew brewing inside my face begins to seep out of my eyes. I smile as hugely as possible; when that doesn't work I fan my face with my fingers. "Wow!" I say. "This is dumb! I'm completely happy for you!"

Melashenko touches his forehead to my temple. *Unspoken rule!* I think. *Personal space impinged upon!* But I don't move. His breath floods my face. It's warm and rich and not unpleasant—a pungency that, I suppose, comes from a legume-heavy diet. I place my hand on his leg. His chapped lips brush my cheek. My nose. My eyes. My forehead. A series of places no other lips have been—not in this particular succession. Then he reaches my mouth, and it's on: his tongue laps against mine like he's thirsty, or like he's a dog licking the floor where a piece of food has once been.

I have no sense of time, only that Melashenko, like a second hand, is moving at a slow and regular pace—one that's practically zombielike. I wonder how long we can keep this up, this dawdling mouth-suction, two sluggards in slow mo. Every once in a while he whispers no or We should stop but instead of stopping his hands find another part of my body to appreciate, parts no one has ever bothered to touch: earlobes, eyebrows, elbows. After what seems like an hour, Melashenko whispers a suggestion: "You can put it down." "It" meaning Beth, our robot child, whose inexplicable hibernation, I'm afraid, might reach its close should I release her, so I say, "No, it's fine, she seems okay right here," thinking, *how many other mothers before me have clutched their infants (and if not real infants, then other things, like satchels, pets, boomboxes) to their bosoms while they made out with their lovers? Is such a chore cumbersome?* It is. But it's also manageable. In fact, it turns out that you can do a lot of stuff while holding a robot baby. You can slide out of your shirt. You can let down your hair. With help, you can get out of your pants. Even your bra. Your underwear, though. Your underwear stays on.

Until it comes off.

"I want to feel you," Melashenko mumbles. Which is

weird, because he's feeling me all over. But then I realize what he means.

"No," I say, gliding toward him. "You're saving yourself."

"For who?"

"The one who you've been waiting for."

"Maybe she's right here," he says, stroking my face. It's clear he's high on his own hormones.

"Don't say that," I say. "It's late. You're not in your right mind."

Neither am I. Because when he says, "Just for a second," I relent. I think, *okay, a second's good, a second's fine, no big deal, in and out, it won't even count, one second is just fine for being one with Melashenko, a guy who I am not allowed to love*! But as soon as he's there, as soon as he's in, it's clear that just a second isn't going to be nearly long enough. *No*, I think. *No*. And when I say no, I let go, because I'm on top and getting off means using both hands to hoist myself up. It's there, in that hoisting, that my letting go commences. It's there, in my letting go, that Beth slips from my grasp and, like a fumbled football, plunks off the railing, through space, and onto the floor, where she emits a siren-like cry, one that starts high, then slows way down to a low, guttural moan, then stops. For a second, Melashenko and I are frozen in place. I have nothing on, Melashenko has nothing on. Our flesh is sticky and exposed to the elements, namely his lamp, which we never bothered to turn off, the one whose shade offers a view of an idyllic scene, cows grazing upon what looks to be an Oklahoman prairie. For a second, I think, *if we lay here long enough, silently enough, time will reverse itself, things will return to normal.*

I've always given Melashenko shit for having all the answers.

What happens when you die? You expire. You return to dust. No heaven? No angels? *Not yet. At least not until the trumpets of the Second Coming wake you from your dreamless slumber.* So what's the point of death, anyway? It's the wages of sin. Why bother with sin at all? *Ask Lucifer. He's the one who wanted to exalt himself above God, he started all this.* So why doesn't God just get rid of him? *Because God isn't interested in creating a universe of automatons, he wanted people who were free to choose their own destiny, free to follow His law, but when they chose not to they transformed the earth into a stage where the Great Controversy between God and Lucifer would unfold and is even now unfolding, where the souls of man can be saved if only they believe in the Son.* "Ridiculous," I'd say, deeming everything he'd said insufficient. It was my way of distancing myself from the fact that it was starting to make sense, that I was starting to like being in the vicinity of one who believed.

Now, though, as I slide my shirt and underwear back on, forego the jeans, and nearly break my neck trying to climb down the ladder, I have a feeling that I might not like Melashenko's answer for why any of this happened, keep expecting him to say something grave and portentous, like, *Our punishment has even yet to begin.* I busy myself with the unsnapping of Beth's pink onesie, while Melashenko retrieves a palm-sized plastic box from a drawer in his bedside table, not because we know what to do, but because we've silently agreed that fixing her will depend upon getting to what's inside. Melashenko retrieves a yellow, tiny, suitcase-shaped box, where there's a collection of miniature tools embedded in black foam. He digs out a tiny Phillips screwdriver and goes to work at the screws in Beth's back.

"Do you know what you're doing?" I ask.

His lips turn inward. "Not really," he says.

"Then should you be doing it?"

"I don't know," Melashenko says.

His fingers work fast, his eyelids blinking urgently, as if to clear from his eyes the fevered dream of our heavy petting. He twists the tool nimbly; finally, the last screw's out. He un-snaps the rectangular plate from Beth's back. Inside, there's a mass of anonymous technology: diodes; tiny cords; a green motherboard, pocked with gold contusions; a microchip, where the evidence of our neglect has been stored and per-haps one day will be played back by Mrs. Jackson herself, as an example for future classes of what to avoid.

"Shouldn't there be like a reset button somewhere?" Melashenko says.

"It's not like she's a video game."

Melashenko places his hands on his hips. "The thing that kills me," he says, "is that there's somebody out there right now who knows how to program this thing. Somebody built this. And now we're at their mercy."

"I could call Ryan Hannigart," I say. "I bet he's up."

The rumor was that Ryan figured out how to hack his robot baby and convinced his partner, Tori Hamilton (a six-foot blond cheerleader with a port-wine birthmark covering half her face), to pull a series of *Jackass*-like stunts. Leave the baby on top of the car, drive off. Put the baby in an old-timey baby carriage, chase it downhill. Walk into a place of busi-ness with the baby in the baby carrier, set it down, leave. YouTube everything.

"No," Melashenko says. "We should fix this ourselves."

I want to tell him that it's no big deal, we're friends who had an accident, it's not the end of the world, plus I'm on the pill and have been ever since Mom took me to her gynecologist after I turned thirteen and requested a prescription of Ortho Tri-Cyclen because, she said, "I know you're going to be curious and you'll want to explore and that's perfectly natural, especially with someone you love and care about, and while I don't want you to interpret this as a green light for having sex with the first guy who knocks on your door, I also don't want to be a grandmother until I'm at least sixty-five."

Instead I say, "You know, it only counts if you finish."

Melashenko doesn't respond. He doesn't say, "That's the most retarded thing I've ever heard" or "Guess what, I already did" or "Is that what I'm going to tell Harriet on our wedding night, that I sank my pole into some chick but because I didn't bust a nut she shouldn't be concerned?" He's too busy fiddling with Beth's lid: spinning it around this way then that, trying to snap it back into place so he can twist the screws back, but nothing's working. I try to think of something jokey to lighten the mood, like Try *mouth-to-mouth* or *Quick, where's a dumpster?*, but what's clear is the mood here is beyond lightening, the mood is giving off a distinctly frantic vibe. Watching him try to reattach Beth's lid is like watching a clumsy-fingered person trying to defuse a bomb whose timer is fast-forwarding to zero. Beth doesn't explode, but something inside Melashenko (i.e., the place where he stores every curse word he knows) obviously ruptures, and for the first time ever, I hear him curse. The chosen profanity (one that describes someone who has relations with one's mother) lingers in the air after he yells it.

The door creaks open. It's Pastor Mel. It's still early (5:15 by Melashenko's clock radio) but he's dressed for church (blue suit, white shirt, red paisley tie), carrying a yellow legal pad and a Bible. Prepping, I suppose, for his sermon. Hoping, perhaps, to stumble upon some material. Well, here she blows. A son in his boxers, a stranger within his gates without pants, a robot baby with a giant hole in her back.

Pastor Melashenko wants to know if we have a minute to talk. We do. We follow him downstairs—*Dear Melashenko, that walk of shame! You with Beth's lid, me with Beth and a hand over her back so her insides wouldn't spill!*—to his office, a room where the resplendent spines of concordances—green with stripes of gold and red—line the walls. I glance around the room, looking for the photo of Dr. M that Melashenko told me about, the 8 x 10 she delivered to Pastor Mel on the occasion of their twentieth anniversary, the one where she's biting her finger seductively, wearing nothing but a lab coat, stethoscope, black stockings, and a black teddy—but I don't see it anywhere, only a painting of a giant Jesus knocking on the side of the United Nations building and a framed cross-stitched message that says *That which is most personal is most universal.* Pastor Mel lowers himself slowly into a blue leather chair, crosses his legs. He folds his hands into the shape of a church and steeple, the latter of which he presses against his lips. After a second he says he doesn't know what was going on in there but that it doesn't take a genius to guess. He shushes Melashenko when he tries to interrupt, then says he knows how hard it is to be teenagers, he was there once, he understands the urges, the desire, but that we have to be so careful, because God gave us these bodies as gifts and what we do with them, well, that's our gift to him, blah blah blah. I want to tell him, "Shut up, can't you see that you're making it worse?" but I don't have the courage, and anyway, the speech isn't for me, it's for Melashenko, who's staring at the carpet as if an extraordinary pageant were unfolding upon its fibers, one in which he's become the tragic star. Instead, I pluck little wires from the hole in Beth's back—*He loves me, he loves me not*—with the full knowledge that this little test doesn't mean anything and that I will end on *not*, which I do, and in my chest it feels as if someone is taking my heart and squeezing it dry.

Nothing ends or begins in the Melashenko house without prayer, not eating, not playing, not waking or sleeping, so of course when Pastor Mel's done explaining how much God loves us, after his eyes have got all watery when he considers how implausibly deep that love is, he suggests that we come to the Lord together. Pastor Mel gets on his knees and Melashenko gets on his knees and I follow mechanically, stuffing Beth into an armpit so we can join hands, and Pastor Mel asks if I want to start.

"I don't know," I say. "I'm not really used to praying out loud."

Pastor Mel has his eyes closed. "That's okay," he says. "Just say what you'd say if you were praying silently."

Right, I think. *Just like in my silent prayers.* I close my eyes. *I can do this*, I think. Just strip down and reach deep. At first, I think maybe I should say something like, *Dear God, please forgive Melashenko and help him forget any of this happened, please be merciful and erase me from his brain*, but then I'm like, *No wait! Don't erase me!*, then *Screw it, do whatever you want, because that's what you'll do anyway, right?* I open my eyes, hoping to catch Melashenko with his open, hoping he'll see me and give me a sympathetic eye roll. But Melashenko's eyes are shut. His brow's furrowed, like maybe he's trying to meditate his way out of this one, as though he's already on some celestial astral plane or wherever Christians go when they lift themselves up.

"Take all the time you need," Pastor Mel says.

The inside of my chest feels like a fireworks display—embers of love and anger and fear exploding then fizzling, then blazing again—and because I can't think of anything to say I shoot a thought beam at the center of Melashenko's forehead: Open your eyes.

Nothing.

I try again: *Open your eyes when I blink. I'll take it as a sign.* A sign? Of what? That we aren't giving up on each other. That we realize we can't be apart!

One of Melashenko's eyelids quivers. I narrow my gaze, imagine I'm burning a hole into his head with my eyes. *Open your eyes*, I think. *And I'll make sacrifices. I'll give up bacon and miniskirts and weed and R-rated movies. I'll don a baptismal robe. I'll trek to the Dark Continent, I'll distribute literature from hut to hut, I'll pop babies out for you, a whole family of future missionaries, to help spread whatever gospel you want, even if it means traipsing through the jungle and running from wild beasts and drug-addled men with machine guns, we will drive vast distances, reaching far-away villages where children will run alongside us, cheering because we have promised to deliver exactly what they need, which is truth and hope and love, which we'll have the power to do because we've accepted each other's diseased hearts and taken them as our own.*

I blink.

Melashenko squishes his lids together tighter. "You're thinking too hard," he whispers. The pulse in his palm beats steadily against mine. A code. A message. It could be the last one he'll ever deliver. And me, I don't have a clue how to read it.

"Just open your heart," Pastor Mel says, "and let whatever's there come out. We're not here to judge. It's just you and the Lord."

"Okay," I say. I know it's my last chance. But I don't open my heart. I shut it up tight. I grit my teeth. I breathe. And then, in the unsteadiest voice, I begin.

THANKS

Thanks to Nic Brown, Phillip Bruso, Austin Bunn, Leslie Falk, Ben George, Alexis Kanfer, Aaron McCollough, Kevin Moffett, and Josh Rolnick for supplying close and necessary readings.

Thanks to Doris Betts, Chris Canto, Charles D'Ambrosio, Nick Halpern, Chris Offutt, George Plimpton, John Ringhofer, Lewis Robinson, and Stephanie G'Schwind for their enthusiasm and support.

Thanks to Khristina Wenzinger for supplying amazing edits.

Thanks to my parents and sister for the ridiculous amount of generosity and support.

And, most importantly, thanks to Kelly and Elijah for their unconditional love.